A <u>He was not reluctnt</u>

CANDLELIGHT REGENCY SPECIAL

Basicly boy meets girl
would have been boring
if not for the Characters.

you'll love Verusel poor guy
loosis out *romanticly* even though he
he was hilareous
No Danger little excitment
3 couples pairs

CANDLELIGHT REGENCIES

THE RELUCTANT DUKE

Philippa Castle

A CANDLELIGHT REGENCY SPECIAL

Published by
Dell Publishing Co., Inc.
1 Dag Hammarskjold Plaza
New York, New York 10017

Dell ® TM 681510, Dell Publishing Co., Inc.

ISBN: 0-440-17234-9

Printed in the United States of America

First printing—April 1981

DEDICATION

*In memory of my mother, radio
writer Margaret M. Lowery, who
knew and willingly shared the
secrets of telling a tale.*

CHAPTER
ONE

Liveried servants skurried, serving maids were cross in their haste, even the grooms in the stables felt the tension emanating from the Hall. Thomas Lionel Everest Brockhurst, Seventh Earl and First Duke of Stanfield, was expected momentarily. Not that the ancient halls of Penwick, home of the late Fifth Marquess of Penwick, and its present Marchioness had failed to be filled with the titled, royalty included, but that when a Duke calls to ask for the hand of the elder daughter, and she a great beauty with a fortune, excitement reigns.

Penwick was built in Elizabethan times and added to over the years so that it ran the gamut from heavily carved oak-paneled rooms to the light, airy Regency style of the present fashion. The Pink Saloon of the new wing was the favorite of all the family, with its delicate French windows, its walls paneled in pink silk, divided by fluted pilasters in gold and white, its mantelpiece of carved Caen stone, its couches and chairs of gilt beech wood, carved with lion-heads and feet, and its Sèvres china in the long rosewood cabinets between the windows. Here hung family portraits, including the first Marquess of Penwick in a piccadill, a cavalier Penwick by Van Dyke, Kneller's portrait of the Third Marquess, Zoffany's group of the Fourth Marchioness and her three children, a Gainsborough portrayal of the present Marchioness when a young beauty and first married, and the latest acquisition—a painting by Lawrence of the high-breasted beauty and elder daughter of the family, Catherine.

The house itself belonged to the Fifth Marchioness, who still ruled supreme, much to the discomfort of her son-in-law, Colonel Hartman. Whether or not he had been a true colonel was a matter of conjecture. That he had money was true; but how he had come by it, no one knew. It was whispered by not a few that his father had been in "trade." Some said a great uncle had had a shady past and had made his fortune on the Continent in an unmentionable manner. Whatever the source, the old Marchioness had put her stamp of approval on him (at least publicly) by allowing him the hand of her only daughter, Clarissa. He had moved into Penwick with his bride, and now his two daughters stood to inherit a great sum.

Other than the mystery about his fortune, there was little mystery about Colonel Hartman. At middle-age he had some trouble with his digestion, a fact which he agreeably shared with anyone who would listen

8

and with some who would not; he also believed, quite counter to his aristocratic surroundings, in Jeremy Bentham's theory of the greatest good for the greatest number of people; and he never tired of talking about economists and philosophers in glowing terms. His only regret was that he did not have a title to match or better that of his ubiquitous mother-in-law. Short, balding, on the plump side, he loved the country, a good meal, and a bottle of port. So it was no surprise when he remained at home with the Marchioness and his younger daughter, Julia, while his wife spent the seasons in London with Catherine, who at twenty had had two seasons out already. This beauty had lacked for no suitors but had disdained to favor any. With joy and some relief her mother now greeted Catherine's interest in the Duke of Stanfield.

On this occasion the family awaited that gentleman's arrival in the pink drawing room, Catherine dressed in white crepe cut in Grecian lines, her dark hair *à la grecque*, curls falling loosely on her high forehead and turning up behind to be caught into ringlets. Tall, majestic, serene, she was the only calm person in the room. Julia, her seventeen-year-old sister, not yet out, skittered from window to window to have a better look at the drive, until her grandmother, the Marchioness, snapped at her to come away and act more ladylike. The mother then took up the post, her hands fluttering in her concern that all would be up to the Duke's expectations.

"A most agreeable man," she commented as she peered out. "A most agreeable man."

9

"You have said that a hundred times already," said the Marchioness, drily. "If he becomes any more agreeable, I shall not be able to stand him."

"Do be good, Mother. You know you must not insult him."

"I shall insult whomever I choose."

"Grandmama, do behave," wailed Julia. "You want him to like us. You want him to propose."

"Do I? I don't know that I do. I haven't yet laid eyes on him, and he is too agreeable by half."

"Don't tease, Marchioness," said the Colonel, patting Julia, his pet. "The child takes you seriously."

"Of course she does. She is the only one with sense in the family."

"Mother, how can you go on so?" chided Mrs. Hartman. "You know you want a title for your granddaughter."

"Do I? I'm glad you all know so much about what I want. It is more than I do. I didn't notice your marrying a title."

"Now, Mother, hush. You know such remarks upset Colonel Hartman. Never could a woman ask for a lovelier husband, I'm sure." She pulled the curtains back to look again down the long drive.

"Humph!" snorted the Marchioness, running her fingers through her hair so that it stood in odd-looking peaks. She was the despair of her maid, who dutifully powdered the white locks a red-brown to match the color of the spots on the King Charles spaniel, then smoothed them into the best coiffure she could manage. Yet, as soon as the Marchioness began to converse with someone, her habitual gesture for emphasis was to run her fingers through her hair, sometimes the fingers of one hand; when aroused, the fingers of both hands, so that she was in a permanent state of dishevel. "Addlewitted," she grumbled to herself, her fingers active.

The natural white of her hair would have softened the inevitable lines of age, but the harsh dye made her expression look hard, her complexion sallow, and her wrinkles pronounced. Much as she hated vanity, she never revealed her age and claimed her youthful look was the result of a glass of vinegar and water each morning upon arising. "People laugh at that dandy Lord Byron and his taking vinegar. I cannot say much for his poetry—a boy showing off, I'd say; wants to shock, but cannot shock one of my generation—but his use of vinegar I can vouch for."

"He is driving up now!" exclaimed Julia, who had made her way back to the window during her grandmother's lapse of attention.

"Julia, do calm yourself." For the first time, Catherine spoke, a tone of reproval in her melodious voice. "One would think you had never before met a Duke." She tossed her dark curls and smoothed the folds of her gown.

"But he is not any Duke. You are in love!"

"*De tout mon coeur*. But pray, don't be vulgar."

"Oh, is that vulgar to say? I am sure I didn't mean it. Only I am so excited. Tell me again, is he handsome?"

"As if I should love him if he were not. At any rate, you will see for yourself *tout de suite*."

"And don't hang out that window, young lady."

11

"Yes, Grandmama."

"You as well, Clarissa."

"No, Mama. Oh, look, Colonel Hartman, what a handsome carriage. Notice the elegant crest."

"It's the horses that are handsome. Finest chestnuts I've seen in a long time."

"Please do come away," said Catherine sternly, so that the three pulled guiltily and reluctantly back from the long French windows as a butler knocked to announce the Duke's arrival.

"I shall meet him," said the Colonel, anxious to leave the women for a few moments. It had not been easy for him in a household of four women.

"We shall wait for him here," commanded the Marchioness.

The butler soon showed in a tall, dark, elegantly dressed gentleman. He wore a dark blue coat, buttoned tightly with brass buttons over the wasp waist, the tails cut off just above the knees and the lapels rising almost to the ears. Just an edge of a buff-colored waistcoat showed, and his white neckcloth was tied in an unexceptionable knot. Buff pantaloons tucked into gleaming black Hessian boots which were cut almost to the knee. His clothes were perfectly tailored and the colors more subdued than was the fashion for many of the dandies. His features, too, lacked the effeminate, graceful look now in vogue. His cheekbones were high, but his nose was long and his mouth large and sensual, giving him a decidedly masculine appearance. Julia immediately fell in love with him.

He bowed, then glanced at the various members in

the room, giving a start as he took in the Marchioness. He quickly gained his composure, went forward, and kissed the old lady's hand.

She smiled. "Nicely done, Duke." That gentleman looked with dismay at the faint stain of red-brown on his fingertips. After greeting each of the others, the Duke was asked to be seated, and tea was brought in.

"I expect the Duke would care more for wine and cakes," said the Colonel jovially. "Wine is better for the digestion. A sound body is the thing. 'A sound mind in a sound body.' Do you fancy the philosophers, sir?"

"I don't consider myself bookish, though I am acquainted with them."

"Nor do I. But I do pick up the masters from time to time. Guides, don't you know. One is in want of superior guides. 'A sound mind in a sound body.' Locke, don't you know. He knew about education without a doubt. Fortunately, I came across him early."

"I wish you had come across him late," said Julia.

"Hush, child," said Mrs. Hartman.

Julia giggled. "But it is so. Because of Locke, Catherine and I had to take a cold bath every day. Cold, mind you."

"That was Seneca, my dear," her father interrupted.

"I clearly collect it was Locke who influenced you, Papa."

"It has done you no harm, surely," said Mrs. Hartman, looking bewildered. "I am sure I thought such a regime better for young boys, but as we had none . . ." She looked at the Duke as though he must understand.

"It has made her a chatterbox," said Catherine, re-provingly.

"Oh, clearly it has not, else you would be one as well." She laughed.

"I must say I have always blamed Locke for Julia's freckles. Notice, Your Grace, she has three upon her nose." Julia turned away in embarrassment.

"I fail to see, ma'am, how Locke can be responsible." The Duke raised his quizzing glass, causing Julia to blush.

"But he advises open air and without a hat or parasol!" Mrs. Hartman exclaimed.

"I don't collect he said *parasol*, my love."

"I am certain he did not, Colonel, for what boy would carry one? Yet I have always said my daughters should use parasols, but to no avail with Julia."

"It would seem, Mrs. Hartman, that your daughters have had a very hearty upbringing." The Duke inclined his head toward his listener. She smiled, discomposed, and put a hand to check her side curls. She was fair, like Julia, with indifferent features and a small, trim figure. Her hands were rarely still, and her mind, apparently as restless, remained with no subject for any length of time. The wine forgotten, she poured tea from a William and James Priest silver pot, the swan-neck spout fluted and chased with foliage. A serving girl passed a tray of scones.

"There is not enough butter on the scones, I fancy," said Mrs. Hartman with concern.

"Better this way," insisted the Colonel. "Hard on the digestion as it is." However, he did not refuse them.

"If you would try vinegar, you'd not have bad

digestion and would look younger," the Marchioness interposed. "Lord Byron has a nice head of hair," she asserted, giving vinegar more powers than that worthy solution perhaps deserved. "Do you take vinegar, Stanfield?"

"Grandmama!" exclaimed Julia, painfully embarrassed by the topic of conversation. Surely a handsome Duke would never need vinegar.

"Don't be so missish, my girl. Comes from her reading too many novels, Stanfield. Life is scones and vinegar, not creaks on stairs and mysterious passageways."

"And do you prefer the creaks to the vinegar?" The Duke referred his question to Catherine, a twinkle in his eyes.

"Indeed, I prefer reality," she said lazily, leaning back and resting on one arm in a pose she knew to be decidedly Grecian. "*Et vous?*"

"I, too," said the Duke, unable to take his eyes from her slender, graceful form.

"Yes. She reads *La Belle Assemblée* and *The New Bon Ton, Magazine*," sneered Julia

"They are quite proper," insisted Catherine.

"And most boring."

"I think not. And they are not what the riffraff read like those common romantic poets you are fond of quoting. Your bourgeois taste appalls me."

"Indeed. And you prefer such remarkable works as 'The Butterfly's Funeral.'"

The Marchioness chuckled and changed the subject of conversation. As the talk went on, Julia could not help but watch her sister. Would that she herself

15

could lean back in just such a pose; but if she tried it, she would only appear ridiculous. How very tragic to be short and round, when one had a sister graceful and reedlike, and to have blond hair, a color definitely out of fashion, and large violet eyes that, although she had practiced the lazy, half-lidded look that Catherine had down to perfection, always managed to look wide and innocent. Julia had tried the Grecian coiffure, but it had only accentuated her lack of Grecian height and grace; so she had had to content herself with an arrangement of full ringlets on each side of her face.

Without a doubt, Catherine was the perfect heroine, while Julia knew that in a novel she herself would be doomed to play the unloved wife.

"Darling Julia, I must have you for my own," pleaded the Duke on bended knee. She looked down on him, her lashes fluttering softly, her bosom heaving voluptuously.

"Answer when you are spoken to, girl. Julia!"

"Yes, Grandmama?"

"Come out of the clouds. The Duke has asked you a question."

Julia blushed and looked at him expectantly.

"I regret having called you from your daydream. I made only an inane pleasantry not worth repeating."

"Oh, by all means, Duke, repeat it."

"Now I cannot think what it was exactly," he remarked, looking, Julia thought, a little bored. He flicked open a gold snuff box and took a pinch.

"Don't let the dog disturb you." The Marchioness

16

referred to her small spaniel who had suddenly awakened and was sniffing at the Duke's boots. "Come here, Beau." The dog went lazily to the Marchioness' feet and yawned. "I call him after the dandy in town, Beau Brummel. That man has such cheek. Who was he? The son of a land agent. Grandfather a valet. He would make a good valet, by God. But a gentleman of society, never. Vain and far too rude. Valets can afford to be rude. They have a reputation to uphold. That won't do for a gentleman.

"Now I think I should like to rest. Dinner is at six. We're on country time here." She arose and swept from the room without further ado. Beau trotted after his mistress, knowing a soft bed awaited him where he could continue his interrupted sleep.

"We must have you shown to your room directly, Duke," said Mrs. Hartman. "I should have let you go at once, but you did come such a short distance, and we were anxious to greet you. Did you enjoy the Kent countryside?" A careless hand again checked her curls. "The woods, though not so majestic as elsewhere, are lovely at this time of year. Myself, I prefer them to the denser woods of other parts."

"But Mother, you have not seen other woods. You do not care to travel," interrupted Julia.

"That is true. Penwick is so charming, I regret leaving here even for Grosvenor Square in season. You are in St. James, I collect?" She smiled at the Duke but did not wait for a reply. "And you have five country estates. Imagine. So you, indeed, are well traveled."

"Yes. Though I find it rather tedious to get about to

them all. Fortunately, I have an excellent estate manager, as I prefer spending much of my time in London."

"Are you a member of White's, and do you gamble at Watier's?" asked Julia, eagerly.

"My dear," corrected her mother, "all gentlemen gamble, but young ladies do not discuss it."

"Why ever not? I think that is very silly. I don't know why young ladies do not gamble as well. I am sure I do with Grandmama. And I often win."

"I begin to think that Julia is too young to come out next season," said Catherine, patronizingly.

"I am not. I shall be seventeen."

"But you know so little of what is acceptable. You will be sure to commit a social solecism. I fail to see, Mother, how you cannot have taught her."

"It's your grandmother," Mrs. Hartman said in despair.

"That's right. Grandmama tells me everything. She says ladies in the eighteenth century were not so missish, that they knew a thing or two. And she tells me; so I perhaps know more than you think."

"Oh, we think you know a great deal," bemoaned Catherine, "except what is acceptable."

"Grandmama says your notions are pure flummery. You know she does."

While this exchange was going on, the Duke raised his quizzing glass to look more closely at this younger sister who appeared so very lively. The mother thought she caught a slight smile on his lips, but what it meant she could not tell.

"I think you will want to see your room, Duke," interrupted the Colonel. "I shall take you myself. We don't stand on ceremony here.

"We have cossetted her, you know," he added as the two walked out.

Julia waited for them to go their way, then jumped up and left the room as well, not wishing to hear any more from her mother and sister. She knew her grandmother would not yet be asleep but would be reading one of the novels which Julia was teased about. In the oldest wing of the house she walked quickly through the North Gallery off which most of the guest bedrooms were situated. She could see the Duke and her father starting up the stairway to the King's chambers. She hurried through the Long Gallery and up a second flight of stairs to the Marchioness' bedroom. Julia and the Marchioness were the only members of the family who slept in this wing, the others preferring the newer, lighter rooms.

She tapped on the door and was admitted by a cross voice. She peeped in and peered at her grandmother, who sat propped up, Beau beside her, in a magnificent seventeenth-century bed with hangings of crimson, embroidered with silver and gold. Chairs and stools matched the bed. Brussels tapestries decorated the walls, and Jacobean oak work set off the fireplace. A dressing table and large gilt-edged mirror stood to one side of the bed. "It is only I, Julia."

"Come in, child."

Julia ran across to the bed and sat beside the Marchioness. Beau licked her, and she tickled his stomach.

"And how did you like your Duke, or should I say Catherine's Duke?"

Julia sighed. "Yes, he is Catherine's Duke, Grandmama. That is just the trouble. I think I'm in love with him."

"Well, think again, child. He is not yours. You cannot have him. Besides, you don't even know him."

"But I know I shall love him even better when I know him, because I am so hopelessly in love right now. It will be much worse."

"Nonsense. I am sorry I encouraged you to read novels. It will be the undoing of you. You cannot just look at someone and be in love with him."

"But, Grandmama, I just did."

"Fiddlesticks. I have taught you more about life than that. Don't you attend to what I teach you?"

"Oh yes, Grandmama." She gave Beau a hug. "But he is so handsome. He is what I have always dreamed of."

"His manners are pretty, I'll grant you. But he seems too much the dandy to me. He is too polished for my blood. I like them rougher, and I had hoped you would as well."

"Oh, he looks very rough to me, Grandmama."

"Nonsense. It is affected the way he holds his head just so as he takes snuff. And he flicks his handkerchief about in a very studied fashion. I don't know that I approve at all."

"I thought it beautiful. He is very right in everything he does, although he does seem a trifle bored."

"It is the truly boring person who appears bored, child. We shall have to observe him more closely."

"That will not prove difficult or tiresome." Julia's eyes sparkled.

"I daresay not, you little puss."

"Have you noticed that he does not talk much?"

"That is no wonder with you in the room."

"Oh dear, did I rattle on? I'm sure I didn't mean to."

"That's all right." The Marchioness patted her hand. "He will have to get used to the family at some time."

"Grandmama, that is not kind. Perhaps, you know, he is shy."

"You are a wise little puss. Perhaps he is."

"And you do approve of him? I cannot believe you do not approve."

"Maybe for your sister. She gives herself airs. They might do. I shall reserve judgment."

"But you will not disapprove of him, surely."

"Do you want him to marry your sister?"

"Yes. I mean . . . Oh dear, what do I mean?"

The Marchioness chuckled and gave her granddaughter a hug. "I can see we may have a problem on our hands. Now run along, child, and let me rest."

"You are going to read. You know you are."

"You interrupted a very exciting part. I'd not put a novel down for everyone."

"I know, Grandmama." She laughed, gave the Marchioness a kiss, and slipped from the room.

"If His Grace the Duke would bend his neck ever so slightly to create an additional crease."

"Thank you, Witherspoon."

The Duke, ensconced in the King's bedroom, was tying his third neckcloth, two already discarded as failures. It was a dark, oak-paneled room once readied for James I, with a suite of furniture and an X-frame

21

chair from that period. Whether the King had actually slept here was a matter of conjecture. The Duke now stood before a large mirror, his valet beside him. He bent his chin to add the additional crease suggested by Witherspoon. That gentleman's gentleman stood, his left arm holding the crumpled cravats.

"Witherspoon, you are invaluable. I understand that George Brummel undertook to take you from me?"

"That is correct, Your Grace. Though how you learned of it, I cannot imagine."

"We noblemen have our secrets and our grapevines as well as you servants."

"Yes, Your Grace." Witherspoon, tall, thin, and beginning to bald, looked on with his usual expression at once bored and patient, acquired by the best of valets to let their masters know they are long-suffering. At times he squinted slightly, and the Duke suspected he was myopic. Yet even so impressive a personage as the Duke would have hesitated taking the liberty to ask.

"I appreciate your staying with me, Witherspoon."

"Not at all, Your Grace. I have been with the family these many years, and under my guidance you have become second only to Mr. Brummel in dress and taste."

"Yet you do not go to he who is number one?"

"Allow me to explain, Your Grace. Mr. Brummel has created his own reputation. I should not find work with him so creative or satisfying."

"Ah, now I comprehend. When I step out, dressed as only perfect taste could attend to, I am a product of your creation."

"That is correct, Your Grace."

"By God, Witherspoon, the old Marchioness is right. There is no comparing a gentleman with his valet."

"Were those her precise words, Your Grace?"

"No, but I gather that was her meaning."

Witherspoon helped his master into a claret-colored coat with matching velvet collar. "Do we remain long, Your Grace?"

"We've no sooner come than you wish to leave. Are you comfortably quartered?"

"Tolerably so, though there are draughts in this wing."

"That's to be expected. But why are you so anxious to get away?"

"It is not that I am anxious to get away but that I was anxious never to come."

"Can it be you don't want a Duchess of Stanfield?"

"I have always understood, Your Grace, that a day would come when a mistress of the house would be necessary. I regret to say that that day appears to be upon us."

"It would seem so, Witherspoon." His Grace sighed. "I cannot say I have been anxious for it myself. Yet when beauty, wealth, and titled family are to be found with one young lady, one must be resolute."

"Exactly so, Your Grace. We shall bear it with equanimity." He sighed as well. "May I ask, Your Grace, when the happy proposal will be?"

"That's more than equanimity, Witherspoon. Next you will be making it a joyous occasion."

"Might I suggest that if it were tonight, we could be away in the morning?"

"Nonsense, Witherspoon. You know as well as I that we must stay a few days at least. I fear it will take me some time to work up to this 'happy proposal.'"

"Yes, Your Grace. Your duel with the Baron of Quigsby seems such a paltry event beside this monstrous task."

"Come, Witherspoon, which is it to be—a happy proposal or a monstrous task?"

"I call it the one and think it the other, Your Grace, and you will never convince me that you are not of the same mind."

"Witherspoon, you know me too well. At least I shall not be bored as I had anticipated. The Marchioness and that young sister should keep me entertained." He put his snuff box into his pocket, checked his pumps through his quizzing glass to insure there was no speck of dust, and stood for a final brushing and appraisal. As he left the room, he turned back. "Don't worry, Witherspoon. I shall keep all in proper perspective. Gambling, horses, then women, in that order."

In the Gallery he met Julia, looking pretty in a white muslin frock trimmed with pink bows. Together they descended to the drawing room to await the six o'clock summons to dine.

CHAPTER
TWO

Dinner that night was in the Winter Dining Hall, a smaller, brighter room than the Banqueting Hall which was dark with carved oak paneling. The Colonel had insisted upon this modern addition as well as some modern touches to the giant old Georgian kitchen. "You know what is said: function is all," he was wont to say. The newer room was pretty with its oval table and rose and blue carpet. The family escutcheon was carved in marble over the fireplace, and a crystal chandelier hung from the white ceiling which was decorated with gold leaf. The Marchioness preferred the old hall and managed to remark on this fact at every meal.

"It is especially lovely for a ball, the musicians playing in the gallery just as in Elizabethan times," Julia added as turtle soup was handed round. The old hall was her favorite room as well. "Perhaps we could have a ball while the Duke is here?"

"The season will start soon enough, and you will be going to many balls, my pet," said her father, soothingly.

"The Duke did not come for balls and routs," admonished her mother. "He has other matters to attend to." She looked knowingly at Catherine, who blushed in embarrassment.

The Duke smiled at Julia. "A ball would be delightful. I should be most happy to attend. That is, if Miss Hartman approves?" He turned to Catherine.

"*I* do not mind a ball," stated the Marchioness, anxious to let it be known who was in authority. "However, it will be more appropriate at some time in the future, not now."

"But . . ." said Julia.

"We'll hear no more about it. They *are* slow about serving the next course."

Soup bowls were removed and fish dishes were placed on the table, each diner taking from that nearest him and offering it to his neighbor as well. There was a freshwater fish with lobster sauce, poached turbot in wine with smelts, an unknown variety smothered in curry powder, and eel quivering beside truffles.

Following the fish came a saddle of mutton, tongue, cauliflower, potatoes, sausage, pickles, braised goose, chicken breasts, and ham roasted on a spit, to name a few of the dishes.

His glass of hock raised, the Colonel toasted the

Duke, on his right. The others toasted in pairs and then drank together. "I hold claret and burgundy thin stuff. Too washy for my taste," the Colonel asserted.

The Duke agreed, admiring the hock.

"You will notice," continued the Colonel as was his wont with every dinner guest, "that the dishes are, if not hot, far from cold."

"Indeed, I did remark that," replied the Duke pleasantly.

"It was for just this that I had the kitchen remodeled."

"And the Winter Dining Hall added," remarked the Marchioness with a scowl. "What the Marquess would think to see us dining here!"

"Yet you will agree the warm food is pleasant, Mama?" asked Mrs. Hartman, nervously.

"I cannot think that I enjoy my food more now. In fact, I am certain I do not."

"Warm food is not only more appetizing but also better for the digestion," insisted the Colonel. "Julia, my pet, that is quite enough hock for you."

"Yes, Papa."

Dinner moved along at a dull rate. The Duke felt a trifle put out as the Marchioness applied herself with assiduity to a small dish of larks in patty shells before he had had a chance to send a servant round to bring some to himself. Beau sat at her feet, receiving the choicest tidbits. The Colonel, despite his faulty digestion, ate heartily with apparently little thought to the food itself, for he seemed satisfied with whatever was directly in front of him.

"My two little songbirds are very quiet this evening," said the Colonel, looking first at one, then the other. Both young ladies were eating daintily and blushed prettily as the Duke's attention was brought to them. "I cannot remember when you two have been so quiet. It is quite a good thing, actually. With so many women in the house, a man seldom has a chance to speak and be heard."

"I look to you to make up a table for quadrille, Stanfield," said the Marchioness. "Or do you prefer whist?"

"Whatever suits you, Marchioness."

"Oh, it don't matter," she insisted.

"Julia will no doubt win, whichever it is," added Catherine. "She always does." The Duke smiled indulgently. It would be entertaining to see a young girl try to win at cards while playing with a noted member of White's.

The main course over, the company sampled pineapple cream, cucumbers in white sauce, spongy cakes, and chocolate soufflé. This finished, Mrs. Hartman suggested the ladies withdraw.

"But we never do," objected Julia.

"Your father and the Duke will want to talk. I am sure they have very particular things to discuss." This with a look at Catherine.

"Nonsense," said the Marchioness.

"But, Grandmother," protested Catherine.

"The ladies in my house never leave the table," the Marchioness explained to the Duke. "I hold that custom old-fashioned and, indeed, quite common. It may

28

do very well for the middle class, but for the aristocracy it don't quite hold."

"You see," said Catherine, making light of the situation, "we treat you quite *en famille*, Duke."

And so they all remained through port. The Duke spoke animatedly of London fashions with Catherine and Julia, of menus with Mrs. Hartman, of Bentham's theory of pain and pleasure with the Colonel, and of lapdogs with the Marchioness, so that that lady decided he was so amiable she mistrusted him and suspected she was in for a boring week or two of being agreed with.

"Grandmother, do you not find his manners unexceptionable and his wit engaging?" whispered Catherine as the small party went into the drawing room for cards.

"Indeed I do, my girl. He has a winning way, so it is no wonder you are taken with him. I notice, though, that Beau don't like him."

"But he had most charming anecdotes about small dogs."

"Exactly so. But Beau don't like him. That is something to be watched. Come along. We'll try the gentleman at whist."

As predicted, Julia won; and the Duke, to his chagrin, realized that she and the old lady were the most formidable players he had yet encountered. Infernally cross at being bested, he found himself in no better humor when a missive was brought in with the evening tea tray. A servant had neglected to hand it in earlier, so that the Duke asked leave to open it immediately, because its contents could be important.

He read his note, folded it, tucked it into his pocket, a stern look on his face. Clearly, it contained bad news; yet with aplomb he entered the conversation, sipped tea as though not a thing in the world had ruffled him, then wished all a good night, though rather early, and went to bed.

The next morning the Duke was up betimes. He took only his morning chocolate, which Witherspoon brought up, then was out to the stables. A ride alone before breakfast would be most agreeable and help him to sort out what he must do about yesterday's missive.

He was startled to meet the Marchioness as she swept out of the stables in a Pomona green riding habit. "I'm on my horse every morning at seven, weather permitting," she answered his startled expression. "You young people spend the best part of the day abed."

He would have made some pleasantry, but she waved him aside. "Get on with your ride, Stanfield. Catherine won't be up for hours, though I'm surprised Julia hasn't joined you." With that she walked toward the house at a brisk rate, leaving the Duke to look after her, amazed.

He entered the stable to find that his tiger had anticipated his arrival. The boy had a decided scowl on his pockmarked face.

"Now, Hoadly," admonished the Duke, "don't frown. You look ready for a role in a Cheltenham tragedy."

"I ain't frownin', Your Grace."

"We already know your animadversions to every country house in the region. Surely, you find little to criticize here."

"Beggin' pardon, Your Grace, but the country is never to my likin'."

"You like it well enough when we're at home."

"Aye, but home is home, as they say; and I—though far be it from me to have a preferment . . ."

"A preference," broke in the Duke.

"As Your Grace says, a preference—but I preference the city."

"You prefer the city. Yes, we know that as well."

"As I was sayin' . . ."

"Oh, don't let me interrupt you, Hoadly."

"How am I to help it when you keep at it, Your Grace?"

The Duke laughed. "Come now, don't look so wounded. What else have you to say?"

"Only what's not my business to say."

"Speak. You will eventually, and will look daggers at me in the meantime. Come now, out with it."

"Beggin' Your Grace's pardon . . ."

"And don't 'Your Grace' me to death. You only do that when you are angry."

"Yes, Your Grace."

"Well?"

"Well, I think we has been well off, so to speak, what with the season in St. James Square and the season in Brighton and some time in the country."

"That won't end."

"No, Your Grace, only we has had a nice bachelor establishment, so to speak."

"In other words, you don't think a lady will add to our present happiness."

"Beggin' your pardon, but me pa always said, 'Them what asks for trouble is them what gets it.' And I ain't never found him wrong."

"Yes. Very wise man, your father. I reflect he had many such sayings, and not one bears criticism."

"No. He was a wise 'un."

Hoadly saddled with alacrity the thoroughbred for which the Duke had paid 1,000 guineas at Tattersell's. As he did so, Julia burst into the stable, her blond curls bouncing. "Oh, Your Grace. Up so early? I am afraid I am too late to ride with Grandmama. She will be ever so cross. You haven't seen her?"

"Yes. She came back from her ride a few moments ago."

"But it is only just past seven. She always goes at seven."

"So she said."

"She must have got the time wrong, though she has never before done so."

"I am sorry you are disappointed. Perhaps you will ride with me?"

"I should be delighted. But where are my groom and the stable-boys? What a strange morning."

"Hoadly will be pleased to help you."

That boy, a wounded expression on his face, saddled Julia's mount and led the two horses outside. The Duke helped Julia onto her gray mare. She hooked one leg gracefully over the pommel and arranged the skirt of her blue riding habit. The Duke had no sooner mounted as well than she was off at a brisk trot.

When they did eventually stop, it was at a pretty stream near a stone ruin. Firs, beeches, and oaks surrounded them.

"A very pretty setting this," admitted the Duke, looking about.

"I call this my Gothic retreat," Julia laughed. "It is too wild for Catherine's blood. She does not fancy the Gothic, as you must know."

"To be honest, I know little about your sister and am come to correct that lack."

"But how can that be?"

"During dancing and over ices and cards one has little chance for other than the latest on-dits."

"Surely you rode in Hyde Park together?" asked Julia, in her interest forgetting the half-lidded effect so that her eyes automatically went quite wide.

"Your sister has many suitors. Time alone with her is quite impossible. No, we have exchanged little else than what is commonplace."

"I think that most tragic."

"*Tragic?* Is not that a strong word?"

"Indeed it is. To be in love, you see, you must exchange intimate notions."

"Intimate?"

"Yes, certainly."

"What sort of notions would those be?" He smiled at her, a tinge of irony in his eyes.

33

She seemed not to notice and explained. "You must tell the person you love something about you that not anybody else knows."

"Such as?"

"Anything that is not commonly known but applies to you."

The Duke looked puzzled. "Would you care to give me an example?"

"Let me think. Well, my grandmama knows this, but no one else. I think, do you not, Duke, that it is all right if perhaps one other person knows—that is, if the other person loves you? Otherwise, I can think of nothing to tell you."

"I am sure that is permissible."

"Good. You will be shocked but must not show it."

"I shall endeavor to be composed."

"Well, I have a page's outfit that I have worn riding very early when no one is about. That way I can ride like a man and go faster than the wind."

"And where did you get such an outfit?"

"From the servants' quarters. That is no great matter. You are laughing." Her mouth drooped, and she looked ready to cry.

"I cannot help it."

"I have told you something very private and very special, and you laugh at me. You will probably shortly tell Catherine so that you can both laugh."

"No. No, truly. I am very impressed with your disclosure. It is just that . . . ," and he commenced laughing again.

She tossed her curls and started to swing her horse about.

"Wait. I must tell *you* something intimate."

"Oh, yes." She could not refrain from showing interest. "That is what you should do."

"All right. Let me think. I know. I shall tell you what is in the letter to me, for I meant to impart its contents to no one. Of course, my sister knows what is in it, because she wrote it."

"That is permissible, since my grandmother knows my secret."

"She tells me that she refuses the man I have planned for her to marry."

Julia looked startled. "What has occurred? Did he offend her in some way?"

"Good God, no. She doesn't want him. Says she must marry for love. The content is pure nonsense."

"You want her to marry someone she doesn't love?"

"What does that signify?"

"But you love Catherine."

"I've just told you, I don't even know Catherine."

"But you came here to know her and learn to love her."

"Actually, I came to ask for her hand. It would be a suitable marriage all around. I hadn't given the idea of loving her a thought."

Julia sat stunned.

"Come, little one, don't look so shocked. There's very little romantic love in this world. In fact, it's all in your pretty head. For my part, I cannot remember ever having loved anyone."

"Not your mother or your father?"

"I didn't know them."

"Not your sister?"

"I feel responsible for her, but I cannot call that love. No, my life has been devoted wholly to my education as a gentleman of title and property, and I have taken the place reserved for me in society. More than that one cannot ask of me. Don't look so sad. Have I caused you to be disillusioned with your fancies?"

"Not with my fancies, Duke, only with you."

She swung her horse about and galloped toward home. The path was pitted, but she was a practiced rider. Little did she suspect that the Duke, praised for his skill, would lame his horse in a rabbit's hole. She glanced back, saw the accident, and reined in her horse. When she saw him pick himself up, she rode on. It would do him good to walk back.

Later that day the Duke was in a black mood. His horse was in bad shape and Hoadly had obviously blamed him. To top it off, Witherspoon was so offended by the ruined boots, he was not speaking. As the Duke paced the North Gallery, he met Julia. "You did not wait for me when I took my tumble," he said cuttingly.

"No indeed, Duke. I keep all in proper perspective. Gambling, horses, then men, in that order." She laughed and ran off before he could respond.

In no mood for conversation, he went to his room to be alone and read a good book, only to encounter Witherspoon. "You will agree, Your Grace, that I do not often show excitement."

The Duke sighed. "Quite correct, Witherspoon. It is fair to say that I have seen you lift an eyebrow only on occasion."

"Exactly so, Your Grace; so that you must be startled to see me so animated at this time."

"It is also fair to say, Witherspoon, that your present animation had escaped me. Do you care to explain it?"

"As it is in relation to your welfare, Your Grace, I think it only proper to tell you. I have discovered a most amazing boot blacking that has not only restored your Hessians, ruined by your fall," he added, a note of disdain in his voice, "but has made them look better than ever."

"I wish you could restore my wounded vanity."

"Your Grace?"

"Never mind. That is excellent, Witherspoon. How did you discover it?"

"In truth, I cannot take credit. Miss Julia brought me the paste and has graciously told me how to mix it, though I am sworn to secrecy."

"Did she, by God? The little vixen. So, she's sorry."

"I had thought it was a rabbit, not Miss Julia that had caused the tumble, Your Grace."

"That's as may be. It was she who hurt my pride—far more delicate than my hide."

"Yes, Your Grace."

"That was not said to be agreed with." He poured himself a glass of sherry. "So, Witherspoon, you have forgiven me. But Hoadly will not."

"I think you are wrong, Your Grace."

"Whatever do you mean?"

"It seems the horse is quite comfortable because of a salve that has been applied."

"You don't mean to tell me . . ."

"I believe, Your Grace, that Miss Julia has a favorite ointment."

"By Jove, that girl will be the undoing of me." He sank into a chair and took the sherry in one gulp. "Men in their proper place!"

"What was that, Your Grace?"

"I hardly know, Witherspoon. I hardly know."

CHAPTER
THREE

No one knew what had caused it. Whether it was the Duke's acquiescence or Julia's pleading, the fine weather (which always put the Marchioness in an excellent mood), or her own fancy could not be ascertained. No matter. The Marchioness decided there was to be a ball at Penwick. The last ball at that country estate had been years before when the Marquess, who loved to dance, was alive. Soon the heavily carved Banquet Hall and Music Gallery of the old wing would be resounding to the lively melodies of the boulanger and allemande.

Julia was the first to be told and could not wait to tell someone. She rushed into the Pink Saloon, very pleased to find an audience of two. The Duke, sitting at a satinwood Sheraton writing table, penning an answer to his sister's missive, glanced up, an appreciative look on his face. "Here's a lovely canary come to entertain us."

Julia laughed and blushed. She wore a yellow muslin dress with a handkerchief front to the bodice and the fullness of the skirt carried to the back of the waist by gores at the sides. Yellow bows adorned her clusters of golden curls at each temple. "You cannot guess, Duke, what is in store for us, and very shortly!"

Catherine, reading *The Lady's Magazine*, whose editorials covered the fashionable chitchat, looked up. She had pulled up her ruby merino dress to show a little more of the double vandyked flounce to her cambric petticoat. "Do calm yourself, Julia."

The Duke laughed. "We're to guess, are we?"

"Yes, but you cannot." Her eyes twinkled, and she twirled about, unable to stand still while he pondered. "Oh, do say something. You are taking an unconscionably long time."

He sat frowning. "I must think this out."

"Julia, do stand still and be ladylike," Catherine remonstrated.

"Won't you guess as well? You will be as excited as I when you know."

"I sincerely hope not, or I shall prefer not to know."

"Oh, Catherine, you will want to know. I promise you. Cannot either of you give a guess?"

"There's to be a card party," suggested the Duke, flicking a speck of dust from his handsome blue coat.

"At which Julia will win," put in Catherine. The Duke gave her a cutting look at that remark. He could not forget such a recent wound.

"No. Guess again."

"I do hate these childish games." Catherine picked up her magazine.

"Come, Duke. Do not give up."

"I shall certainly not do that. But come. You know me well enough to call me Thomas." He ignored Julia's blush. "I know. There's to be an *al fresco* nuncheon."

"What a clever idea." She clapped her hands. "We could have it by my Gothic ruins. Oh, but that is not the surprise."

"You are to have a new horse."

"No, no. This is for all of us."

"For all? Let me think. What rhymes with 'all'? Could it be 'ball'? Will there be a ball for all?"

"You are clever, Thomas." Catherine broke in.

"You knew!" Julia accused him, pushing her lower lip out as she did when vexed.

"You should not have asked him to guess if you are to be angry when he is right."

"He is teasing me. You knew all along, Duke. Admit it."

"I must confess my guilt."

"But how? I am the first to know."

"Hardly, as I knew before you."

"Impossible, unless you practice sorcery. Grandmama said I was the first to know, and she would never mislead me."

"My girl, you are the first of *us* to be told by your grandmother, but you are forgetting the servants. Her abigail told my valet who told me only a quarter of an

41

hour ago. It is a communication system not even God could improve upon."

"Oh . . ."

"Do not say it," remonstrated Catherine. "She tends, Thomas, to say things young ladies should not say."

The Duke laughed. "I don't doubt that."

Julia gave a sheepish laugh, then ran over and sat down abruptly next to Catherine on the settee. She gave her sister a hug. "We must make plans."

"From what I understand, the Marchioness has already begun," the Duke commented.

"You know Grandmother will take complete charge." Catherine had ceased reading and toyed with her curls.

"You are right. But we shall make suggestions," said Julia.

Catherine laughed. "I doubt that they will be taken."

Julia laughed as well. "She is sure to think of something far greater than we. Duke, I mean Thomas, you will meet everyone around."

"Everyone who *is* anyone, my pet," Catherine corrected her. "Ho hum, I fear we shall have to ask Lord Newbury. A frightful bore," she explained to the Duke. "He commits puns."

"We shall have musicians and ices and little cakes . . ." Julia, ignoring her sister, went on in her own vein.

"I wonder what I shall wear," Catherine mused. "Perhaps something new."

"There will be no time to have it made up. I think your sarcenet skirt trimmed in ribbons and net would be lovely."

"That is rather pretty. I shall think about it."

The doors were opened, and the Marchioness entered, her hair in any number of odd peaks, proof that she was already at work planning the coming fête. "Children, I hope you are all pleased with my news."

"Delighted, Marchioness." The Duke stood until she had seated herself on a delicate needleworked chair.

"Of course you are. It was you who wanted a ball, I collect."

"Indeed, we all did, Grandmama."

"You did, puss. I am certain of that." She chuckled.

"Grandmama, tell us what balls were like in the hall in the old days."

"Humph!" snorted the Marchioness. "The *old* days? It was only yesterday that the Banquet Hall was lit with candelabra. I had flowers put everywhere. I never did care for the barren rooms of the great houses. No. Flowers everywhere and colored lanterns in the garden.

"Of course, in those days, not so very long ago, mind, we had elegant fashions, not the silly little wisps you call ball gowns today. We had billowing skirts sweeping the floor, and trim waists—mine was eighteen inches until I had your mother and it went to twenty—never forgave her for that. Can't be more than twenty now." She smoothed her dress to show her waist. "But with today's fashions, who's to know? And the men were not the pudding-hearted things of today. Why, the cicisbeos I had. . . ." The Marchioness ran her sentences together so that her speech had a decidedly peculiar rhythm, and it was difficult, if

43

not impossible, to stop her progress. That is, if one dared.

"'Child' (the Marquess always called me *child*, for I have always looked so young for my age)," she smoothed a peak or two of her hair. "'Child,' he would say, 'you are ravishing tonight as always.'" She had a faraway look in her eyes, and all were silent in regard for that not so long ago past.

"Grandmama," Julia had the courage to break in, "I think the flowers sound lovely. I hope we shall have them for this fête."

"Naturally, puss."

"It will be so very Gothic!"

"Gothic?" snorted the Marchioness. "I should think not. Gothic, indeed. It is very *me*. That's what it is."

"But, Grandmama, it is Gothic to be picturesque."

"Well, we ain't being picturesque. We're being elegant."

"It is very fashionable to be Gothic, Grandmother," said Catherine lazily, giving the Duke a knowing look.

"Is it?" asked the Duke with a smile.

"Indeed, yes. We go back to the picturesque in nature—rustic cottages, ruins . . ."

"What is picturesque about an old cottage?" asked Catherine, laughing.

"There's something so inspiring about what is rustic."

"Can't see that," snapped the Marchioness. "Never could."

"Grandmama, it uplifts one's mind. Why, even this house we are in, even this room, has sublime significance."

"Now, now, puss. Visit your Gothic ruins or put up your rustic shack in the garden, but don't bring the sublime into my drawing room, if you please. I haven't been so bored since tea with Lady Blightley.

"We had better think of guests. I suppose the usual from these parts. Girls, we shall put you to work on the invitations."

"Oh, Grandmama."

"Now, puss. Balls are work as well as play. To have the one, you must do the other."

"It will be my first ball, Duke."

"It is difficult to see that," her sister said drily.

"Oh, Catherine, I shall not be as bored as you at my eight-hundredth ball, at my nine-hundredth ball, at . . ."

"That's far too many balls," put in the Duke. "You will be swept off your feet before your tenth ball, marry a handsome lord, and settle down as a married lady."

Julia looked stunned. "Indeed, I shall not. I shall not marry at all if it means that." She laughed and twirled around the room. "I shall dance my life away and never stop. Years from now people will say, 'Who is that old lady who never stops dancing?' and they will be answered, 'She started dancing at the thought of her first ball and has never been able to stop.'"

The Marchioness grabbed her. "You are forgetting the part of the story in which the wicked grandmother comes and assigns the waltzing lady the horrifying task of penning invitations. The spell is broken, and she will never again dance her life away."

"Oh, Grandmama. You spoiled a lovely thought."

"I'm sure. Young ladies, you have your work before you. Stanfield, come with me. We shall look at the old Banquet Hall together and decide how best to arrange the furniture. When I give a party, I oversee everything."

"I shall help."

"You will write, Julia. I should like to get to know you better, Stanfield." She took his arm. "Come along."

Julia longingly watched them go. The Duke, although dressed as a Corinthian, displayed the virile figure of a sportsman. Julia felt almost dizzy anytime she was near him. But she was in constant consternation; for if he looked at her, she felt weak, and if he did not, she was in despair.

Ball plans progressed at a hectic pace, with the Marchioness in her glory. Mrs. Hartman was sure a ball before the season and with Julia not yet out was not the thing. She was often forced to seek her vinaigrette as monstrous problems arose, only to be dealt with head on by the Marchioness or by Julia, both of whom welcomed anything out of the ordinary. Catherine took refuge in her boudoir where she supervised the fitting and sewing of a new ball gown which she must have. The Duke took to long rides in the woods.

Shortly after the gilt-edged invitations were sent, the day arrived. An awning erected over the front drive was Catherine's contribution to plans. The last of the pots of flowers were brought to the Banquet Hall, while the head butler directed maidservants in the laying of the best table linen in the new dining hall, and footmen carefully polished crystal and set the table for twenty with priceless hand-painted china. The small group would dine at eight before one hundred arrived for the dancing.

Musicians tuned their instruments. They would play during supper in the new dining hall, then move to the Musicians' Gallery in the old hall, long used as a ballroom.

Julia was the first to enter the Pink Saloon and await the dinner guests. Busy with ball plans, she had not troubled about a new dress but wore a gown with bodice of pink and skirt of blue tulle over a pink satin slip. The dress had a rounded neckline, tiny puffed sleeves, and a border of scalloped lace. Julia's abigail, Lettie, had outdone herself in arranging the golden hair. It was caught up behind in a braided circlet and curled into ringlets on the forehead. Julia peered out the long windows, then toyed with objects on the mantlepiece. Would the guests never arrive!

The Duke entered, and Julia swung about nervously. He stood for a moment surveying her. She could not help being aware of his manly figure which was shown off by the waisted coat with long tails, black satin knee breeches, black stockings, and dancing pumps. His thick chestnut hair had been carefully combed by Witherspoon to fall casually on his forehead.

"You are looking very lovely tonight, Julia."

She blushed. "Thank you, Duke, I mean Thomas."

He laughed. "That's better. I've not seen much of you lately, you have been so busy arranging our fête. I appreciate all the work you have done and the time

47

from riding and other entertainments it has cost you."

Julia beamed. She had never felt so delighted. "But I have loved every minute of it, Thomas. Grandmama and I are capital at giving parties. Why, only last year we gave a rout that was much talked about."

"I can believe that. Tonight, I am sure, you have surpassed yourselves."

"We have." Julia had a disarming way of admitting the truth, good or bad, so that she did not feel the usual awkwardness with a well-deserved compliment. "You have enjoyed your long rides about the country-side?"

"I should have done so far more with you to accompany me."

"Yes. I can see that. What a pity Catherine does not care much for riding. She looks splendid upon a horse. I have not seen her ball dress, for she means it as a surprise, but she told me it took an amazing number of hours to make and fit. And, of course, she wished to supervise. She says in London she need not trouble about a seamstress. I am sure I cannot wait to go there."

"But didn't you want a new gown for your first ball?"

"Oh, yes, if it could have appeared by magic, but not if I must take the time that Catherine took. Goodness, we should then not have had the ball. Anyway, Norval—Lord Devon as he loves to be called, you've not yet met, but he has accepted for tonight—Norval told me at the rout last year that I look ravishing in this gown."

"And quite true."

48

"Nonsense, Thomas." She twirled around to show it off. "It is not so very unusual, and I could not look ravishing even in Catherine's new gown. Norval, you see, doesn't know what 'ravishing' means. I am convinced of that. But he has good taste and quite liked the gown, so I thought it would do."

"I like Norval already, and his good taste. I am convinced he most certainly does know what 'ravishing' means."

She blushed as Catherine came gracefully into the saloon. Both occupants stared at her. The new gown was dramatic, the green and scarlet satin clinging to her as she moved. The neck was cut in a deep V and the back, which could be seen as she walked majestically past them to stand by the window, was cut low.

Julia suddenly felt very ordinary and wished she had spent time on a new gown. Thomas could not take his eyes from Catherine. And little wonder. Julia felt angry with Norval. Ravishing, indeed. She would never forgive him for saying so. She might have had a new ball gown that Thomas could admire.

"Here you all are." Mrs. Hartman came in with the Colonel, who sat by the fire and lit a cigar. "Julia, I do not know that I am at all happy about this ball. You know, you have not yet been out. What will Lady Jersey say when she hears of it? If you should be refused admission to Almack's, I could never show my face again. I am sure I do not know why we are giving it. I thought I had said that we should not."

"Now my dear, do come and sit down. This will be a fine affair, once supper is over. Can't think why we are having some to supper. Bad for the digestion to eat a meal, then dance. That's right, sit here and relax." Mrs. Hartman joined him by the fire. She checked her reticule to be certain it contained her smelling bottle.

"I cannot think why the guests are late," she said, nervously playing with her handkerchief. "Cook will be very angry if we do not serve on time. You don't suppose the musicians will play too loudly at supper, do you, Colonel? Julia, you are not to dance the waltz, remember. One of the ladies at Almack's must first give her approval."

"Yes, Mama. I shall endeavor to remember."

"And do not be rude to Norval when he arrives."

"I'm sorry he has returned from Vienna in time to attend."

"What a naughty thing to say. I cannot think what possessed the boy to go traveling. He no doubt means to be a man of the world."

"You mean his mama wants him to be."

"Norval a man of the world?" put in the Colonel. "Not very likely. Never studied the philosophers."

"Papa, he takes great pains not to be bookish."

"Well, he needn't. Couldn't know what the books were about if he read 'em."

"You are both unkind to poor Norval. And the two of you make such a lovely pair, Julia dear."

"But Mama, he follows me about like Beau does when the poor dog is sick."

"You see, he cares for you."

"Norval is interested in no one but himself."

"That is not true, I am sure."

"And his food and his dress. He does look quite the thing. And his title. We must not forget his title."

"You see, he has many interests. You are too hard to please, my dear. What is a poor mother to do, Colonel?"

"I am quite anxious to meet this Norval," said the Duke, in an aside to Catherine. "Yes," Catherine replied, "Lord Devon is quite a dear and so fine a match for Julia. I do not doubt the silly girl will change her mind once she has come out."

At that the Marchioness entered, causing some present to gasp. She swept into the saloon in a lavish ball gown from earlier days. It was of pale brown satin that went well with her red-brown hair. The square neckline was exceedingly low with bunches of cream-colored lace at the bosom. "If I am to waltz—and do not look so shocked, daughter, for I mean to try the waltz—I shall look as a lady should look," she announced. "Stanfield, I hope you stand up with me. We'll make a handsome couple."

"Delighted, Marchioness." His lips twitched.

"Mother," exclaimed Mrs. Hartman once she had adjusted to the Marchioness' attire, "I have just been telling Julia how well she and Norval look together, and she persists in making unkind comments."

"I don't blame her. The boy's a foolish puppy. If she can't do better than him, she'd do better not to marry at all."

"Oh, never say such a thing, Mother." Mrs. Hartman looked bewildered. "Not to marry at all. Dear me. I am sure you should not encourage her as you do. Oh, what is keeping everyone?"

"How I wish," sighed the Colonel, "that it were to-morrow morning and all the guests were at home and nothing unforseen had occurred. I don't doubt I shall have indigestion."

The first of the guests to arrive, to Julia's chagrin, was Viscount Devon, the ubiquitous Norval. He entered with a dark, bearded stranger.

"Hope I'll be forgiven for bringing an extra guest. Doctor Linse." He presented the doctor to the family. "Just arrived unannounced from Vienna. Couldn't not come, could I? Couldn't leave the doctor neither. Dilemma, what?"

"You did the right thing, Norval," said Mrs. Hartman, frowning. No one in the family could bring themselves to call Norval, who had grown up with Julia, "Lord Devon."

"Delighted to welcome you, Doctor," said the Colonel, heartily greeting Dr. Linse. Mrs. Hartman did not look so very delighted and gave a whispered order to the butler, who hurried away.

The doctor greeted them, a slight German accent to his carefully spoken English.

Aside to the doctor the Colonel commented, "We're sure to have a lively discussion once the dancing is underway. Do you favor the philosophers?"

The doctor gave an ambiguous smile and said nothing. He was a small man. His dress was subdued and his manner, formidable. He seemed to Julia not so much to be greeting the present company as to be observing each in turn.

Other dinner guests arrived in their finery. At any time the Marchioness could draw on a guest list of the cream of society. But for tonight and Julia's first ball, she had kept to those houses not too far distant.

Soon the supper party was assembled in the new dining hall. Julia found herself seated between Norval and Lord Farthingham, whose conversation was entertaining as he went on about the scale used for bags of coffee at Berry Brothers, on which Beau Brummel had weighed himself with and without boots and frock coat. "It is said," remarked His Lordship, "that the Prince Regent himself has sat on that scale."

It was time for Julia to turn reluctantly to Norval. She tried with great effort to discuss something meaningful, but to no avail. Norval was all very well in his way, which, she had to admit, was slightly odd. He was of medium height, certainly taller than she. He had pale brown hair and a pale complexion and had taken to wearing an eye patch over his left eye that he said was weak and needed rest. He dressed in the latest fashion and looked far more interesting than he actually was. She had known him for as long as she could remember. They had played children's games and robbed birds' nests and ridden their ponies wildly about the countryside. It was hard to take someone seriously as a beau that she had bested at sports all her life. Julia had been the leader in all their mischief. But as he got older, his mother instilled in him what it was to be a Viscount, so that he was becoming, to Julia's mind, decidedly stuffy. What is more, he no longer tolerated her teasing, for she had once done her best to upbraid him when he took himself too seriously. Just when the adults of both families were deciding that she and Norval made a delightful

53

pair—no one had thought so as they whooped their way around the countryside—Julia was deciding she had had enough of Norval. The Marchioness was the only one who agreed with Julia, while their mothers' heads were full of foolish notions.

Julia noticed that Doctor Linse, who sat opposite her, still seemed removed, even while talking. His black eyes looked dispassionately from one guest to another.

It seemed to Julia that he watched the present company as though they were all guinea pigs in his laboratory.

"Observing my mentor, are you, the good Doctor Linse?" asked Norval, handing Julia a dish of pineapple cream.

"Your mentor?"

"Yes." He looked very pleased with himself. "Attended his lectures in Vienna. Brilliant man."

"And on what did he lecture, pray?"

"Animal magnetism. He's a colleague of the famous Doctor Mesmer."

"I have heard of *him*." Julia's eyes lit up. "Does Doctor Linse know how to mesmerize?"

"Right up to crack. Gave demonstrations. Was mesmerized myself."

"No. You, Norval? Weren't you frightened?"

"Not in the least."

"But someone else has power over your will. I shouldn't like that."

"Not at all. Simply relax. Your inner mind gets the suggestions."

"Yet that is what is frightening."

"No. Won't react unless you want to, Doctor Linse claims. One of the first to make that claim."

With difficulty Julia did not succumb to being rude by talking across the table to the astonishing doctor, though she longed to question this strange, formidable man. Maybe he could read her mind. His eyes certainly seemed able to pierce some protective level of those he gazed at. Julia found him fascinating. "Maybe he will mesmerize me!"

"Can't say."

"Maybe I can learn to mesmerize."

"Rubbish. It's not for girls to learn. You have to do anything new you hear about, Julia."

She laughed. "Norval, you know me too well. I must certainly learn to mesmerize. Did you learn to do it, Norval?"

"Should have, don't you know. But I find I don't attend to studies. Entertaining, those lectures, but as to working at it, well . . ."

Julia sat back, disappointed. Not to learn animal magnetism when one actually sat in on the lectures! How foolish. It sounded like something Norval might do.

Supper was soon over, and Julia and Catherine were greeting their young friends who arrived for the dancing. Julia was soon promised for most of the dances, and Thomas had not yet made her a request. He and Catherine were elegant leading the group in the opening dance. Everyone exclaimed how well they looked together, tall and graceful. Julia had to be satisfied with Norval. She noticed all the gentlemen but Norval had trouble taking their eyes off Catherine. Even Doctor Linse had escaped from the Colonel and stood watching Catherine, his small black eyes all-observing. At the moment, Julia was not so sorry that Norval was her partner. At least someone was noticing her.

A country dance with Lord Mayfield followed, then a waltz. Julia was annoyed at having to sit it out but got great pleasure in watching the Marchioness, still graceful, waltz with the Duke. Julia drank claret cup and chatted with Norval, who to her mortification had worn his eye patch tonight. "Do be sensible, Norval, and take off that ridiculous patch. It isn't as if you needed it."

"I most certainly do need it."

"Nonsense. You just want people to think you have been wounded fighting in France, while everyone here knows you and knows you have never been to the war."

"I might have been but for my duty to my title and family. It won't do for the head of a great house—and believe me, I feel the weight of the responsibility since my father's death—to get himself cut up. Anyway, mother would worry frightfully." He had a happy thought. "She quite approves of the patch."

"I daresay, if it keeps you happy."

"I wish you were as concerned about my happiness, Julia."

"Well, I'm not. You have too many people, including yourself, concerned with it already. Come, Norval, do not pout. Someone must tease you."

"I suppose you think it is good for my character?"

"Decidedly."

"So you *are* concerned for my welfare."

Julia choked on a swallow of her drink.

"I notice you are free for the allemande," said a soft, deep voice behind her. Julia turned to see Doctor Linse staring at her. She was free and had been hoping Thomas would ask her, but he had not. How did this strange man know? She could not help but blush slightly. It was certainly exciting to think of doing German dances with a Viennese mesmerist. She was sure very few young ladies could claim that pleasure.

The black eyes watched her as she glided through the steps. "I should like to learn to practice animal magnetism." Julia came straight to the point as they danced. She hoped one would not have to attend lectures in Vienna, for a young lady would never be allowed to do such a thing, even if her parents agreed.

He laughed for the first time, his mouth curling to a sardonic smile but his eyes remaining alert and serious. "Young ladies do not practice animal magnetism."

"Why not?" She was disconcerted. No one had ever before told her she could not do something.

"You have your own duties in life to fulfill."

"I cannot think it is anyone's *duty* to mesmerize. My mind is very good. I am told I learn quickly."

"Yet it is for a man to work with the will of others."

"Pooh." Julia could not help but think of Norval initiated into these wonders. "I think you are unkind."

"Dance and be merry, little lady. And forget about

mesmerism. I shall teach my secrets to no lady. The female mind simply cannot learn them."

The Marchioness, had she been by, could have told the good doctor that he had unfortunately said quite the wrong thing. No one had ever been known to dissuade Julia by saying *cannot*. In fact, the word acted as a spur to a horse, driving her beyond all reason. By the time the allemande was over, she was firmly decided. She would learn to mesmerize. She had almost forgot her partner, the doctor, as she imagined herself already a mesmerite, soon to practice the wonders of science on the mind. If this foolish little man would not help her, she would see what she could discover in books. Or she would find another doctor from Vienna. There must be more than one. Surely they were not all in Austria. She would find another who graced the English scene.

The next dance belonged to Norval. Julia smiled on him with more favor, and he beamed back. He would be an excellent subject on which to practice animal magnetism. She would start with Beau, then work up to Norval.

When Julia had despaired of ever seeing Thomas again, he appeared at her side. She gave a little gasp and fanned herself nervously.

"This dance is mine, I believe."

"But, Duke, you have never requested it."

"You are free?"

"Do you, too, practice mesmerism?"

The Duke laughed. "I leave that for others." His eyes danced.

He led her to the floor to make up the fourth couple in a quadrille. Catherine was partnered by Lord Farthingham. Those two looked handsome together, the dark and the fair. Ah, well, thought Julia, any man standing up with Catherine looks his best. She looked up at Thomas. His sensual mouth belied the scornful smile it often took on. What a mystery he was. He smiled at her. "You are a very graceful dancer."

"Thank you." She smiled her broad, frank smile but noticed he was now watching Catherine. Thomas will soon be Catherine's, she thought sadly. Yet as she watched, she noticed that Farthingham, as well, kept his eyes on her sister. No one noticed Julia. She supposed she would go off to strange lands, as other Gothic ladies had done, and practice something edifying.

The couples finished their five figures, the strains of the quadrille died away, and Julia was not sorry to see it end. Her partner had not been hers. She quickly curtsied to the Duke and went in search of Norval, who was to be her partner for the next set of country dances. He was nowhere to be seen. Tired of dancing, she wandered to the billiard room. Here she found her father and Doctor Linse playing at billiards.

"There is a pagan spirit abroad in the world," the doctor was saying as he tapped the ivory ball but missed a pocket.

"I'm not entirely with you there," said the Colonel, taking his turn. "To my mind, material things are quite good for us. That is, if everyone's got 'em. Too much is in the hands of too few. 'The greatest good for the greatest number of people,' I always say. You can't go wrong with Bentham, don't you know."

"Yet, Colonel, you will always have the few who

59

prosper and the many who struggle. I hold with the older monastic approach, though I'll grant you not so much from a belief in God as from a belief in the mind's controlling itself. Transcending any condition. That would sum up my creed."

"Indeed no. That couldn't be mine at all. Everyone should partake to the fullest of all that's good here. Your monastic approach smacks of what Bentham would call 'hoary antiquity.' It's today we're in, not yesterday, not some future heavenly state or not even your transcended mental state. Things must be fashioned with today in mind."

The doctor glanced at the opulence surrounding him. "Then you would have to share all this and give up much. I notice you have not yet done so."

The Colonel cleared his throat. "Things move slowly, you understand. Only an idea at present. Has to catch on. Anyway, property's not mine to dispose of." He gave the cue ball a heavy hit and was far wide of his mark. He then lit a cigar and was silent for several minutes, looking glum. He was not aware it was his turn again, so Julia, who had remained unnoticed, slipped over and took his cue.

"Thank you, pet. Yes, that's right. You play a little. She's very good, Doctor. Taught her myself."

The doctor smiled indulgently. "I fear I am considerably ahead of your father. Do you choose to start a new game?"

"Not at all. I am merely substituting. I hope the stakes are high."

"Not as high as I could wish, considering my position." He smiled ironically, and Julia laughed.

She took her turn. Doctor Linse, standing lazily by, was notably impressed. "Beginner's luck?"

"No beginner that one," said the Colonel. "Mediocre shot for her, I'd say."

Julia, miffed at the pompous doctor, miffed at Thomas for ignoring her and at Norval for deserting her, although if she were honest with herself at the moment, she would have to admit she was glad he had, set to the game with a vengeance. One by one the balls were pocketed. Doctor Linse gave a long whistle as she cleared the table and won the game without letting him have another turn.

"I am now glad the stakes are low."

"Well you might be." Julia reeled around at that remark to see the Duke watching and laughing. After her first surprise, she had to smile. "Would you like a game with me, Duke?"

"Not a chance. I cannot afford to continue losing to you, Miss Hartman." He gave a mock bow.

"Nonsense. You know you are wealthy and own five estates."

"That may be. It is my ego that cannot handle another beating. The good doctor here will agree with that, I am sure. He looks as if he is suffering from the same sort of wound."

The doctor failed to reply as Catherine entered and remonstrated, "Here you are, Julia. How very unladylike. You should be upstairs dancing."

"Why so should you, for that matter. I doubt that I have been missed."

"I am sure Norval is searching for you."

"That is always a safe remark, sister. I suspect if he wanted to, he could find me. You have."

"Come, you are out of sorts."

Flushed, Julia gave a quick curtsy to the doctor, thanked him for his game, not without reminding him that as loser he stood in her debt, and ran out to the garden. In the coolness of the evening she felt refreshed. But she was more determined than ever to learn to mesmerize. Somehow she would force that odious doctor to teach her.

She turned around as footsteps approached to see the Marchioness sweeping grandly toward her. The old lady surveyed her, then put an arm around her shoulders. "You don't look so very happy, puss. Ain't you enjoying your first ball?"

"Oh, yes, Grandmama. Truly, it is lovely. Only . . ."

"I was afraid of that 'only.' Almost kept me from having the affair."

"Don't say that. We should have had it."

"Yes." She patted the girl's shoulder. "Nothing's perfect, even one's first ball. But we wouldn't miss the excitement of any of it, would we?"

Julia laughed sheepishly. "No, certainly not. Only I mean to get that dreadful Doctor Linse to teach me to mesmerize."

"Do you? Then I daresay you will. Against it, is he?"

"Totally. He absolutely refuses."

"That sounds final. Of course, he hasn't come up against you before."

"Not until the game of billiards."

The Marchioness chuckled, a deep crackling sound. "How much is he indebted to you?"

"Not much, yet."

"Since he is staying with Norval, we must challenge them to cards tomorrow evening."

Julia's eyes twinkled. "What a splendid idea. Would you suggest whist or loo?"

"Quadrille's the thing, my child. You always shine at quadrille. Let me see. Doctor Linse, Norval, you, and me. That's our four. We'll make our opponents wish they'd never seen us or that deck of forty cards."

Julia clapped her hands. "Grandmama, how can we wait?"

"By dancing at the moment. Run along inside, child. Norval's no doubt looking for you."

"Did someone speak my name?" Norval came down the path, his unpatched eye not yet accustomed to the dark so that he groped his way toward them. The Marchioness smiled, and Julia tried to suppress a giggle.

"There you are, Julia. Marchioness." He saluted her, then turned back to Julia. "Your mama sent me to look for you."

"You mean *your* mama. She is out of sorts whenever I am not dancing with you."

"Well, she fancies you. Quite a compliment."

"I daresay. You disappeared for the country dance we had together."

"Oh that. Thought I'd have a little read in the library while you was dancing and fell asleep. Wasn't gone long, though."

"Ho hum. Norval, how can you fall asleep during a ball? You used to have a little more life to you."

"You see, a little magazine reading is always a good thing—catch up on the gossip—and then the cares of being a Viscount weighing heavily upon me . . ."

"I do tend to forget that."

"Mustn't forget it. Best thing about me."

"Yes, Norval, I think you are right. I shall endeavor to keep that in mind."

"Off with you, children."

"Grandmama, come inside. You will get a chill in this cool air."

"Me? Come now. Run along. I have a little remembering to do. This is not the only ball to warm this old house and gladden this old heart. I should like to be alone now with a few ghosts of the past."

"No ghosts," said Norval. "Some said Sir John of Peasely once walked here but hasn't been seen in centuries. Don't mean to disappoint you, but you won't see ghosts, Marchioness."

"I'll see what I choose to see, young man."

Julia patted her grandmother's hand, then led Norval to the hall. She glanced back to see, standing on the lawn, the silhouette of a grand eighteenth-century lady.

"Won't see no ghosts." Norval shook his head.

The ball ended, but before the family retired, the Colonel gathered them together in the Pink Saloon. A servant had brought in champagne and at a signal from the Colonel, poured it out and passed the glasses.

"We must have a toast before retiring," said the Colonel.

"Yes, it was a lovely ball, Papa. Thank you ever so much." Julia could not help sinking onto a sofa.

"And a special ball," said Mrs. Hartman. "Tell them, Colonel."

He cleared his throat. "Thomas has done us the honor tonight of asking me for Catherine's hand." He raised his glass. "To a long and happy marriage."

The Marchioness gave a start. The Duke took Catherine's hand and the two smiled at each other. Julia felt faint and could only watch the bubbles in her glass and hope she would not cry.

"Isn't this lovely?" said Mrs. Hartman, wiping her eyes with her handkerchief.

"Indeed," said the Marchioness drily. "This has come sooner than I expected. You surprise me, Stanfield."

"I surprise myself, Marchioness. But Catherine looked so fair tonight, I could not help but declare myself to her."

"*Inutile de vous dire*, I could not help but respond favorably," Catherine added with a light\laugh.

"When is it to appear in the *Gazette*?" asked the Marchioness.

"Oh, not until the season," replied Catherine. "The announcement will gain much more attention when we are all in London. It will be quite a lark—all the good wishes, the *soirées*."

"Yes, well then, it is not to be official until the season commences. And you approve of delaying the announcement, Stanfield?"

"Of course, Marchioness."

"So do I. This gives you a chance to get to know each other better. There's no scandal in crying off as long as it's not official."

"Oh dear, surely they will not change their minds, Mother?"

"Of course we shan't," insisted Catherine.

"Just want to be sure everyone is happy. I always say, Stanfield, that I don't believe in hurrying things along."

"I'm sure I never heard you say that before, Mother. Quite the contrary, I should think."

"Well, I'm saying it now and shall continue to do so. See that you attend to what I say. Poor puss, she's almost asleep. I'll wish you much joy and take her off to bed."

The Marchioness took Julia's champagne glass and set it down, then bustled her out of the room before any attention could be given to her.

"And I thought romantic Julia would be so delighted," complained Catherine. *"C'est dommage."*

"Dead on her feet," said the Colonel. "I doubt that she knows we've made the announcement." He chuckled. "How she enjoyed her first ball."

The doors shut, and the Marchioness and Julia, their arms around each other, walked slowly and silently to the old wing.

"Julia, you have shown a decided impatience to get to cards this evening. What is in that devious mind of yours?"

"Hush, Catherine. You embarrass me. You know I always enjoy a game with Grandmama."

"I know you like to pick up spending money from our guests. I do not think it in good taste. I think gambling is for men."

"Pshaw!"

"And do not make that disgusting sound."

"Grandmama does."

"We are all aware of what Grandmother does. That does not mean you need do it."

"And you are not to tell me what to do."

"Girls, girls." Mrs. Hartman fluttered up to them as they entered the Pink Saloon. "I do not know why you cannot get along like those two lovely daughters of Lord Wellesley."

Julia giggled. "Their mama tells them they should be like Catherine and me."

"Well, she cannot know you, I'm sure. What is the trouble now?"

"I find it ill-mannered of Julia to win money from our guests," Catherine announced so the others could hear.

Doctor Linse and Lord Devon were already seating themselves along with the Marchioness at the card table. The Duke stood by the fireplace, filling his pipe. Colonel Hartman, despairing of a good conversation if games were to be played, had retreated to the library.

Julia scowled at Catherine as Mrs. Hartman said, "Quite right. I forbid you to do it again, Julia."

"Clarissa, don't be foolish," snapped the Marchioness. "We always gamble for a little. Gives spice to the game."

"I am sure Catherine is right, Mother. I simply cannot have the child taking money from our guests. I must forbid it." She looked at Catherine for approval.

"But Mama!" protested Julia.

"Dear me, I wish the Colonel were here."

"We don't mind gambling at all," said Doctor Linse.

"Like to gamble," put in Norval.

"No. It isn't seemly. That is, we do not think it is seemly." She glanced at Catherine again.

"Come and play, child." The Marchioness was already shuffling the cards with deft fingers which any man at White's or Watier's would appreciate.

Julia sulkily took her place. Their entire plan was spoiled.

The Marchioness waited until those not playing had seated themselves at the far side of the room. "I think," she announced, "that we must gamble for something. What will it be?" She had a twinkle in her eyes that Julia recognized.

"I do not mind losing a few shillings to the young lady," said the doctor, patronizingly. "Nor I," added Norval. "Dashed good fun to gamble, what?"

"No. Money is out for Julia, so we must think of a substitute. Let me see . . ." she paused, but the others could think of no satisfactory solution. "I have it. We shall make a promise to do something that it is in our power to do for the winner."

"I warn you, I usually win," said the doctor. "I must say, I find your suggestion delightful." He looked at Julia and smiled.

"Damned exciting," said Norval. "Excuse my language. I get carried away with games. Usually lose. But might win sometime." He looked around the table with his one good eye. "Though don't expect to tonight."

"That leaves you, Julia. Do you agree?"

"Well, Grandmama, it might be a little unfair." She looked down, blushing and holding back a smile.

"Have no fear," consoled Doctor Linse. "We would not ask anything of you that would displease you."

"Then by all means, I must agree."

"It's settled then." The Marchioness dealt the cards with such dexterity the good doctor watched in disbelief.

As the evening wore on, the doctor looked disconcerted, then decidedly angry. "Are you certain, ma'am," he asked stiffly, "that this is the usual quadrille deck?"

"Bad *ton*." Norval took umbrage. "Decidedly bad *ton* to say that, even to think that."

"Oh, no offense," the doctor added quickly. "I only meant you ladies play as though you were magicians."

"Not at all," said Julia lightly. "We are only poor females who do not, as you do, know the secrets of the mind."

"Just the cards," said Norval pleasantly, because he was used to losing to these two. The Marchioness chuckled. "Dashed good game, this," he went on, "though I can't say I like losing with the bet that's on. Never had an experience like this one."

"That does it, gentlemen," announced the Marchioness grandly, after all but the Duke and those at the card table had gone to bed. "Julia has won."

"She plays well for a young girl," the doctor commented, but he did not smile. "What little thing would you like us to do for you, my girl?"

Julia looked at both men. "Let me think. I shall first ask Norval to support me in making any request I shall make."

"Glad to. Would have done that anyway. I like this game of yours, Marchioness."

The doctor smiled sardonically. "And shall I support you in this mischief as well?"

"Oh, no, I think not. It is of you I shall make the request. I shall require you to teach me how to mesmerize."

70

"Impossible! I have already explained." The doctor was furious and looked to the Marchioness for support. "You will agree that this request is intolerable, ma'am?"

"Highly unusual, I should say, but then so was our wager. She won fair and square, you know."

"Well, I shan't comply with that request. Make another."

"Not pay a gambling debt? Bad *ton* again, Doctor. I must support Miss Hartman. Promised. Though I'd do it anyway. Must pay a debt. Put gambling debts before anything else. Needn't pay your tailor or bootmaker but must pay your gambling debts."

"This is tampering with science. I'll not honor such a plan."

"Then," said Norval forcefully, "I must call you out, sir. I invited you to this house and must see that you act honorably. And I warn you, I am an excellent shot."

"Come now, this has got out of hand. Do not forget, you have been my student. The lady will make another request of me won't you, my dear?"

Julia smiled sweetly. "No."

"You see, she won't. Am I to call you out?"

"Certainly not."

"Then you must teach her."

"I never heard of anything like this."

"You had a free choice to agree or not before we started," put in the Marchioness. "I'm afraid, sir, you now have no choice. Julia, pick your time."

"Tomorrow morning at ten."

"Then tomorrow morning it is, Doctor."

"And I shall be there to see you do it, true to my debt. Although I must say, I wish you had picked to-morrow afternoon, Julia. A fellow likes to sleep."

"Then," said Julia happily, "it is all arranged."

The Duke, who had been reading, sauntered over to the table as the group broke up. "What is this I hear about an arrangement? What is to occur?"

"Gambling debt, Duke. My good friend and mentor, Doctor Linse, demured at paying, so I'm forced as my debt to call him out if he don't pay."

"Surely, if there's some money involved . . ."

"No money, Duke," Julia said sweetly. "A favor only. You see, the good doctor is going to teach me how to mesmerize."

The Duke laughed. "So that's it. Have you ever not got what you wanted, Julia?"

"Never."

"I have agreed most reluctantly. I call it tampering with science. At any rate, it was a decidedly strange game."

"Careful what you say, or I must call you out," reminded Norval.

"Really, Norval, there is no one like you for wanting a duel. Just because you're the best shot around," said Julia, her eyes sparkling.

"Nice of you to say so."

"Not at all."

"But you do see my position is awkward?" insisted the doctor.

"Decidedly," agreed the Duke.

"One shouldn't teach secrets of the mind to a young lady."

72

"Naturally."

"So you support me in this?"

"Certainly not. You must pay a gambling debt."

"Told you so. I did explain it, Duke. You're a fine man, Doctor Linse, but you ain't got the rules down, don't you know. Must go by the rules."

"Exactly so," said the Duke. "I am afraid, Doctor, there is nothing for you but to begin your lessons promptly. I am sure," he turned to Julia, a faint smile quivering on his lips, "you have a very apt pupil."

"I'll say good night, then." Doctor Linse arose from the table and walked from the room without further ado.

"Not up to snuff, that one," said Norval with a shake of the head. "Brilliant doctor and all that but not up to snuff. Almost sorry I brought him. Hope I'll be forgiven."

"Oh, we are very pleased he has come," said Julia brightly. "And you paid your debt to me handsomely."

"You thought so, did you? Glad of that. Like to be of service. Only sorry I can't duel but would hate to injure my mentor. Wouldn't do."

"No, not at all. It has turned out quite happily."

"Yes, puss, as I said, you always do rather well at quadrille."

The next morning at ten, Julia met with Doctor Linse and Norval in the study. The doctor had pulled the curtains so that the room was in darkness.

"Oh, my," she said upon entering, "this seems so mysterious."

"I want you to know, young lady, I highly object to

73

what we are doing. If it were not for Lord Devon . . ." He did not finish his statement.

"I agree. We are most fortunate to have him with us. How kind you are to take part, Norval."

Norval blushed. "Glad to be of service." The doctor glowered at him. "Don't look so sour, Doctor. She won't remember all this any better than I have. Safe as can be, your teaching her."

The doctor did not seem to like the remark, but did not answer. He solemnly turned to Julia. "Be seated, please." She did so, awaiting further orders. "First, Miss Hartman, you must understand what we are undertaking. A little history would not be out of order. The great Doctor Mesmer understands about the universal fluid that ebbs and flows within our bodies."

"Universal fluid," said Norval absently. "Seems I've heard of that before."

The doctor glared and went on. "Some force is in action, you understand, like the moon controlling the tides of the sea."

"She don't understand at all, I'll wager. I never did."

"Quiet! Magnets have just such an attraction for things they don't actually touch. Therefore, the great Doctor Mesmer has theorized that the heavens' magnetic influence affects the nerves. It is safe, then, to assume that there is a magnetic force within our own bodies. This theory led the great man to use magnets at first. Later he realized *he* acted as the magnetic force as he touched the patients. This he termed *animal magnetism*."

"Never used magnets with me. Didn't touch me neither. Went right out, like a candle. Did anything you said. Quite a lark."

"Do be still. Later, Doctor Mesmer became aware he could merely point a finger to be obeyed, though he continued to cure with music and the laying on of hands.

"I, however, employ a different device. Instead of music, I use my voice to induce a mesmeric trance. You are already succumbing to it. I have been speaking in a monotone and very, very softly. Your body is relaxing. Your arms are limp, your legs are limp, your back muscles are limp." The doctor's voice droned on and on. "So comfortable, so pleasant.

"Now it is difficult to keep your eyes open. You try to keep them open but you cannot. You shut your eyes. You are growing more and more tired. You are drifting, drifting, drifting. . . . You go deeper and deeper.

"Now you will listen carefully to what I say. Listen carefully. You will never mesmerize anyone. You will never again want to know anything about mesmerism. Any time you hear about animal magnetism, you will change the subject. You will forget the game of cards we played. You will forget everything you have done so far this morning. Forget. Forget.

"When I count from five to one, you will begin to wake up. When I reach one, you will be wide awake, having forgot this entire experience. Five, four, three, take a deep breath, two, and now you will open your eyes and you will have forgot, one."

Norval stretched and yawned. "What are we doing

75

in this dark room? Fool place to be. And why are the curtains drawn?"

The doctor gave a rare little laugh. He walked to the windows and drew the curtains back. "Yes, we need some sunlight. Miss Hartman, have you been riding this morning?"

"Every morning, Doctor. What an impressive demonstration. Norval went right out as he said he would."

"You don't mean . . . ?"

"What are you talking about, Norval went right out? I did no such thing. What has been going on?"

"You were mesmerized, Norval."

"What? What's that? I think we should change the subject."

Doctor Linse could not help but laugh. "Doctor," said Julia reprovingly, "Norval is your student. Now he remembers nothing. That is quite serious."

"I'd say there's been no great change."

"But he went all the way to Vienna and studied with you."

"Vienna? Who went to Vienna? *I* never did, I can tell you. Come to think of it, I can't think what you're doing here, Doctor, though I remember bringing you. Did I know you before?"

"I taught you about mesmerism."

"Well, let's not talk about it. Duced dull, this. Ain't we going on a picnic or some such thing?"

"Yes, the others must be ready. Thank you so much, Doctor. I have observed you carefully. You quite repaid your debt."

"I shall be more careful in the future."

"Yes, do. I think you were unfair to poor Norval."

"Oh, I don't mind, Julia. Glad to have brought him, I'm sure."

The family and their two guests had gathered on the steps. There was to be an *al fresco* nunchoen at the Gothic ruins. Julia hurried to join them after changing to her riding habit. She, Catherine, Thomas, and Norval would ride while Doctor Linse and the others took the Marchioness' carriage, an elegant one that turned the heads of many during the season in London. It was gilded on the outside and trimmed inside with pale blue satin. Two bewigged footmen rode behind. They did so today, wearing their blue satin livery. "You look straight out of the eighteenth century, Grandmother," Catherine complained as usual, to which the Marchioness retorted that she *was* straight out of the eighteenth century. "It's as good a time as any to be straight out of. Can't think this century compares. You're all too missish. And the men are such dandies. It must take Norval's valet an hour to squeeze him into that riding habit. And a different colored eye patch to match every coat! I hate vanity."

"Do hush, Grandmother. I think he looks quite the thing. He and Julia are lovely together."

"Are they, Catherine? Glad to know you think so. Purple eye patch!"

"Of course, he's not a Duke."

"That's the main difference?"

"Well, certainly. It would always be preferable to be a Duchess. One wouldn't pass that up lightly, would one?"

77

"No. *One* wouldn't."

The riders went to the stables to choose their mounts. "I do hope cook won't forget the food," worried Mrs. Hartman. "And did you remind the servants about the china and crystal, Mother?"

"Everything's under control. Benton will follow with the lunch."

"The claret." Colonel Hartman was ready to jump from the carriage.

"Taken care of, Colonel." She signaled her coachman to drive on.

The carriage of necessity kept to the paths, whereas the riders could canter through the wild woods, carpeted in leaves. Julia and Norval rode behind Catherine and the Duke, Catherine looking striking in a scarlet riding habit that set off her black hair. She had insisted, much to Julia's consternation, on riding the black stallion.

"Can't see why you're worried. Your sister can ride what she wants," Norval remarked.

"You forget, Norval, that she does not ride often, nor does she ride well."

"She looks smashing on that horse."

"That is precisely why she picked it."

"He's a sweet goer."

"I think you are not supposed to notice that."

"Can't see why. Not jealous of your sister, are you?"

"Certainly not. How can you, Norval? I am convinced, however, that that is precisely what the Duke thinks."

"Then stop making a cake of yourself and let her make her own decisions."

"But she's such a goose about horses. That one is very tricky. He's even hard for me to handle."

"Puffing yourself up a bit, ain't you?"

"No, I am not. That's a high-couraged animal and she'll be heavy-handed with it."

"Not your concern, that. Duke's mount is a handful. Shouldn't like to see either of you on that. Shouldn't like to ride it myself."

"You needn't worry."

"I say, can't think why I brought that doctor along. Rum sort of fellow, what? Wonder where I met him." Julia didn't answer. "Well, no need to pout. Think I'll ride up with the others. Supposed to be a pleasant outing, this." He whooped at his horse and rode up behind the others.

"No, Norval. The stallion's skittish!"

But it was too late. Startled, Catherine's horse bolted. She screamed, unable to hold him back. The Duke took after her with Julia not far behind. Norval joined in the chase as well, thinking it all good fun.

Julia was worried that Catherine in her fright would forget to duck the low branches. Fortunately, her sister had enough presence of mind or maybe instinct to keep her head down. As Julia had feared, the horse shied at the first fence. Catherine might have been able to take the jump. Instead, she was thrown over the horse's head and into a field that bordered the wood.

As the Duke rode up, the stallion suddenly reared and struck at him, knocking him to the ground.

"Norval, get the stallion under control," Julia yelled. But Norval had dismounted and climbed the fence to help Catherine, who sat bruised and crying. Julia dismounted, patiently coaxed the nervous stallion to her, then tied its reins to the fence.

She turned, expecting some sardonic comment from Thomas, who had had time to brush himself off after his fall. He would be angry about this. Instead, he lay where he had fallen. His own horse had bolted and stood at a safe distance.

"Thomas!" Julia ran to him where he lay facedown, unconscious. She rolled him onto his back, then shrank back, gasping in horror. His face had hit the gnarled root spike of a tree. It was so bloody on one side, Julia could not tell precisely where the wound was. It looked as though one whole side of the face had been ripped away. Not knowing what else to do, she tore up her petticoat with trembling hands as unchecked tears rolled down her cheeks. She bandaged his head in an attempt to stop the bleeding. While she tried to revive him, she could hear the others at the fence.

"What a cocklebrained thing for you to do."

"I couldn't help it, Norval."

"Yes, you could. Needn't have ridden the stallion. Could have told you so."

"Norval, you didn't tell me. Julia did."

"Then you knew."

"Do stop scolding. I thought I could handle him." Then she gave a scream as she saw Julia bent over the Duke. She rushed up. "What has happened?"

"He's badly hurt. We shall have to act fast. Catherine, you take Norval's horse and go to the ruins."

"I say, I don't like her taking my gray."

Julia ignored him. "Tell Grandmama to bring the doctor to the nearest path in her carriage. I hope he practices medicine. Norval, you and I must get Thomas onto my horse, and I shall take him to the carriage."

The two were too stunned to object further and meekly followed her orders. With Norval's help, Catherine reluctantly mounted his gray and left for help. Norval and Julia with great difficulty lifted the still unconscious Duke to Julia's steadier mount. He lay across the saddle, Julia mounted behind.

"Norval, you ride the stallion back to the stable and tell Hoadly to come for the Duke's horse. Well, hurry!"

Norval, no mean horseman if he put his mind to it, had no trouble calming the stallion and galloping toward Penwick.

By the time Julia reached the carriage, she was certain Thomas must be dead. Under the Marchioness' supervision, her father and one of the footmen took the lifeless form from the horse and placed the Duke in the carriage, his bleeding head in the Marchioness' lap. "Hurry!" the Marchioness commanded. Julia and the Colonel climbed in as the old lady directed the coachman to drive with all possible speed. "The jolting won't bother him, and he must get to a doctor."

"But where is Doctor Linse, Grandmama?"

"It seems the good doctor gives lectures and practices mesmerism only. Claims the sight of blood makes him faint." She gave a sniff.

"I should have sent Norval for Doctor Hugo."

"No need. I sent Danvil for him on Norval's gray. Scared nearly out of his satin livery, poor fellow. Well, what was I to do? There now, don't cry, child. Time enough to cry when we know the damage."

"But Grandmama, you haven't seen . . ."

"Bloody face always looks terrible. Might not be as bad as you think."

"Your grandmother's right, you know." The Colonel patted her hand. "Probably just a bad knock on the head."

"But where's Catherine?"

"Humph," the Marchioness snorted. "Had a case of the vapors. Couldn't bear to see him in pain, she said. Your mama's administering to her, and Doctor Linse is attending only too conscientiously. Silly girl would just be in the way with her hysterics. It's better she didn't come."

"Poor Catherine." But Julia said this rather absently as she chafed the Duke's hand.

"Don't try to bring him around, child. He's better off not feeling this bumpy ride."

Danvil had ridden well, for shortly after the Duke was carried to his room, Doctor Hugo arrived. Witherspoon, so startled about the wound that he did not even concern himself with the damaged Hessians and blood-smeared riding habit, took charge of his injured lord. The doctor shooed all but the trusted valet from the room. Even Julia, sure she could help, was forced to leave. But she remained outside the door, pacing the hall like a caged animal. The Marchioness, seeing it was useless to try to calm her, took her arm and paced with her.

At a time when minutes seemed hours, it was many, many minutes before the doctor emerged, looking very grave. "Serious, I'm afraid, My Lady. A concussion for sure. Hopefully not a fracture. The left eye is all right, but the face is torn up pretty badly. He'll have a nasty scar. Can't be helped," he added to Julia's helpless protest.

"May I see him?"

"He's unconscious. There'd be no point."

"Please?"

"I suppose so. His man is with him. I'll look in again shortly."

Julia tiptoed to the bed and stood beside Witherspoon. Thomas lay as though dead, half his head swathed in a fresh bandage. "I shall help you nurse him," she whispered, the tears starting again in her eyes.

"Yes, Miss Julia. I should be glad of your help," he answered kindly. He had thought well of this pert little lady ever since she had come to the rescue of the Hessians. Now he was glad to sense one who shared his deep concern for his master.

"We shall pull him through this, Witherspoon. Have no fear."

He smiled at her. "With you here, Miss Julia, we are sure to do splendidly."

CHAPTER
FIVE

The family found it difficult to induce Julia to leave the sickroom. The Marchioness sent for her at tea time. Pale and forlorn, she entered the drawing room. Attired now in a dainty sprigged muslin, she sipped her tea silently and ate a biscuit only upon the Marchioness' insistence.

Catherine found her own release in verbally chastising herself for taking the stallion. "This need never have happened."

"All right, my girl. That's enough. It was a corkbrained thing to do. We all do corkbrained things from time to time. Couldn't be helped, and I don't want you blaming yourself. No one else blames you."

"Norval does. He said so." Catherine's eyes were red.

"Rum thing to say. What were the Duke and Norval about, letting you ride that horse?"

"Thomas didn't know I do not ride well."

"If he paid attention, he would. You never get any practice. Must have seen that. And it was addle-brained of Norval to allow it. If he'd take off that eye patch and look at what's going on! Like to get my hands on that boy. Viscount, indeed. Head of a family, hah! Now drink your tea. Go on, both of you. Can't have you two moping about. Got to show a little courage. We weren't so faint-hearted in my day."

"Is there someone we should tell, Grandmama?"

"I've been thinking about that, puss. He has a little sister, don't he? I expect she'd like to come and help nurse him or cheer him up. There's no mother or father, I collect."

"Just a horrid governess. At least Thomas doesn't say she's horrid, just a dead bore, which I should think would be horrid," said Julia.

"Dead bore, is she? Can't have that. Nothing worse. Shan't have her here then."

"But, Grandmother, you must," protested Catherine.

"Well, I shan't. I shall fetch the child myself. Anything she needs to know *I* can teach her."

"The governess will insist upon coming," said Catherine.

"To me? Don't be foolish. She'll do as I tell her. Who wants to make the journey with me?" Neither girl spoke up. "Catherine, I think you had better come, as you are the elder."

Catherine sighed with relief. "Oh, yes, Grandmother. I think I should at that."

"Anyway, I know how you hate a sickroom. Julia, I trust you'll tend to things here."

"I shall, Grandmama."

"Then that's settled. Well, run along, child, before you fidget yourself into a state. Catherine, you and I will pack for an overnight stay. I have already sent a message ahead to expect us. Harriette, I think, is her name. Shouldn't wonder if she'd be upset. I'll depend upon you to calm her down. And no more blaming yourself. Understand?"

"Thank you, Grandmother. You can depend on me." She walked over and gave the old lady a hug.

"I know I can. Always could. You come up to snuff after some sniffling." They both laughed.

Julia suggested to her mama that a room be readied in the old wing next to her own. From what the Duke had told her about Harriette and from the way he sometimes compared his sister with Julia, she suspected that Harriette would appreciate the room she had picked. Julia put her own favorite novels and poems on the bureau and cut and arranged the flowers herself. She was convinced she would like Harriette and could hardly wait to meet her. If Julia were not cast down about Thomas's injury, she would be in excellent spirits. He was not recovering as quickly as expected. Although he had regained consciousness, he was delirious at times and fretful, so that she and Witherspoon were hard pressed to keep him quiet. Julia feared the wound was infected, for he ran a fever; and she sat by the bed for hours, bathing his head in vinegar water. Poor, poor Thomas. She feared his pride would be as injured as his head when he was able to recall the circumstances of the accident.

By late afternoon of the third day, the Marchioness had returned with her charge, and Julia was introduced to a small, shy, very pretty brunette with delicate features. She was dressed with unexceptionable taste in a primrose pelisse and matching French bonnet with a plume. Grunby, the Marchioness' abigail, took these garments from her, and Julia admired the white cambric dress with a full flounce of white lace. On Harriette's feet were scarlet morocco slippers.

"Might I take Harriette to her room, Grandmama?" Julia asked as soon as the introductions were over.

"She must be allowed to compose herself," agreed Mrs. Hartman, making the two girls laugh.

"Run along, then," said the Marchioness. "Harriette, I have instructed Grunby to show your abigail to the servants' quarters."

"You are so kind, Marchioness." Harriette spoke softly.

"Kind? Never been called 'kind,' " she grunted. "I've been called many things, but never 'kind.' I fancy I'm quite a tartar when crossed. Consider yourself warned."

Catherine and the Marchioness joined Mrs. Hartman in the saloon while Julia, laughing and shaking her head, led the bewildered Harriette away.

"How is my brother? Your grandmother said there has been improvement, but what does that mean?"

"I shall take you to him after I show you your room. Witherspoon is bathing him at the moment. I must tell you the truth. He is sick from fever, and we have been trying to keep him quiet because of the concussion and the wound."

"How bad is the wound? From what the others did not say, I gather it is terrible. Catherine literally shrinks when it is mentioned."

"Doctor Hugo assures us it will be much less evident as it heals. He says all wounds look horrifying to start with. Doctor Hugo has seen men in battle, so he must know."

"I do hope he is right. My brother is so very handsome. I wonder, will he be disfigured for life?"

"We must not think that. The wound might look very distinguished, like a German fencing scar."

"Do you think so? I am very much relieved."

Julia did not think so, because she had seen the open wound, but she felt that Harriette needed time to get used to what had happened. "You were whisked away in a great hurry. I hope you were not too shocked."

"I could not think what the Marchioness was about, sending a message that she would arrive almost at once. I must confess I was quite frightened of meeting her. My governess, Miss Marmion, a tedious old lady, said that the Marchioness was known as a terrifying woman. I was quite beside myself until she arrived and was ever so kind."

"Well, you must not tell her so again, or she will get cross. I understand she is the terror of London society, and she will not want her reputation ruined. Everyone bows to her wishes, even the ladies at Almack's."

"I think she likes me a little," Harriette ventured shyly.

"I am certain of it. I mean to come out next season

and I hear that you do as well. I know that Grand-mama will be most helpful."

"You mean we are to come out together? How exciting." Then she looked pensive, her smile fading.

"What is the matter? Do not worry. Your brother will surely be fine by then."

"As soon as I come out, I must announce in the *Gazette* my engagement to Lord Effly."

"Are you already engaged?"

"Not exactly. Thomas would have it so. He and Lord Effly have an understanding. Miss Marmion says I am very wicked to defy my brother. In truth, I cannot defy him. But I have objected strongly, and he will hear nothing I say."

"That is unthinkable." Julia pondered a moment. "Is Lord Effly truly odious."

"Oh, he is worse than that. He is old, at least past thirty, and he is partly bald and takes huge pinches of Nut Brown, sneezing abominably—his fingers are stained with it. He talks of nothing but the affairs of his estate. He drinks too much port and gets blear-eyed after dinner. Oh, I could go on for an hour about all that offends me. You will find him abominable."

The girls stood in the hall of the old wing, so anxious to converse they had not yet entered Harriette's room. Julia opened the door and led her inside. "I hope you like old things. Grandmama and I do. And I have put out my favorite novels for you."

Harriette rushed to the bureau and read the titles. "I am so delighted you read novels, too. What a grand collection."

"I hope you have not read them all."

"No indeed. Miss Marmion disapproves, so I am forced to snatch time in secret for reading."

"Read all you like here. Grandmama does as well."

"I am so glad. And you fancy Lord Byron's 'Childe Harold'!"

"I find him so romantic."

"I too." She spun around and examined her room. "This is a very mysterious room." There were two crimson and gold damask high-backed chairs by the fire, a heavily carved four-poster bed with crimson velvet covering and curtains of gold brocade with a heavy fringe.

"What a good word for it. You are right. Though it will not frighten you?"

"A little. That makes it more exciting. Are there secret passageways?"

"One that was boarded up long ago—right here by the fireplace. But have no fear; it cannot be used."

"Still, it adds flavor, does it not?"

"I am glad you feel that. If you should be uneasy, my room is next door."

"I shall love it here." Then her expression was sad once more. "If poor Thomas were not injured, it would be quite perfect."

"I thought that myself. But I shall leave you alone for a moment then take you to him."

Julia went to her own room and lounged on the bed. How very strange of Thomas to want his sister to marry such a dreadful man. Money and title could not mean that much, especially since Thomas himself was so wealthy. This did not sound like the Thomas she cared for. Her head spun. It was all so confusing. She did like Harriette, who was just as Julia had imagined she would be. What I must do, thought Julia, is meet this Lord Effly as soon as the season starts. Then I shall know better how to deal with him. I am sure that Thomas does not see him as disagreeable. Nevertheless, Thomas should not force Harriette into a match she abhors.

She soon led Harriette to Thomas's bedside. The girl turned pale when she saw her brother, moaning and restless, half his face swathed in a bandage. Witherspoon sat beside his lord, bathing his head. The valet greeted Harriette but did not leave his post. "I shall relieve you directly after tea," Julia told him. She conducted Harriette out and toward the Pink Saloon.

"It is much worse than I had feared. What shall I do?" Harriette wrung her hands.

"You must not fear. He is progressing nicely. After some refreshment you can help me nurse him. Then you, Witherspoon, and I can take turns."

"And Catherine? Is she with him often? I like her so much. She has been very thoughtful of me."

"Catherine has always been frightened of sickrooms, so Grandmama thinks it is just as well that she stays away until he is somewhat better."

"She is overcome with her sorrow!" exclaimed Harriette. "How very tragic."

"Yes," said Julia. "I think Catherine does not show what she feels, which makes her a very romantic figure."

"Just like a character from a novel. I thought that at once. And so beautiful." The two girls sighed.

* * *

Julia ran down the hall and burst into her grandmother's room. "It's Beau, come quick. He's in a
trance."

"Beau has never been in anything else, child. Do be
still. I am at a very exciting part."

"But, Grandmama, I've mesmerized him. It worked.
You must come and see. Only . . . ," she paused.

The old lady looked up. "Only?"

"I cannot awaken him."

"That's not surprising."

"Grandmama, you do not understand. This could be
serious. What if he remains mesmerized?"

"Can't hurt him, I'm sure."

"Do come." She pulled the Marchioness out of bed,
along the hall, and to her own room. There was Beau
on the bed, just as she had left him. "You see. I shall
try again to bring him out of it. I was really rather
good at getting him under, once he stopped jumping
off the bed and scratching. But I have practiced for
hours using a low, calm voice. Now, Beau, I shall
count from five to one. When I say 'one,' you will
awake. Five, four, three, two, and now you will
awake, one."

Beau did not move. She ran over and shook him,
but he slept on. "Whatever shall we do?"

"If you want him off your bed, and he shouldn't be
on that velvet cover, I'll call him. Beau!" The dog
jumped off the bed and ran to his mistress.

"He *was* mesmerized. He was just waking up when
you called."

"Fiddlesticks."

"I think I was a great success. I shall prove it. I shall mesmerize you."

"You'll do no such thing."

"Please, Grandmama."

"Don't 'please, Grandmama' me, puss."

"Do you not wish to know what is in the inner reaches of your mind?"

"I do not. Quite satisfied with my mind the way it is, thank you. Go work on Norval. Get him to take off those colored eye patches."

"I have had him in mind. He seems to be mesmerized quite easily. You, I am convinced, would be difficult."

"I should think impossible."

"Yes, it would be very good for Norval to do away with those silly eye patches. At any rate, I am convinced I had Beau in a trance."

"No great achievement that. If he lifts his leg and notices a leaf, he forgets to put the leg down. You've no conquest in Beau."

The old lady left, and Julia, tired of animal magnetism for the moment, sought out Harriette in Thomas's room. The Duke's fever had died down, so that he now had long periods of quiet sleep and could talk a little to his attendants when awake. Julia found him fast asleep and Harriette in a chair nearby doing needlework.

"Is he all right?" Julia whispered.

"As usual," Harriette answered in a low voice. "I think we do not need to whisper, because he sleeps very soundly. I suspect there is laudanum in the medicine Doctor Hugo left."

"Perhaps. I am so relieved that the restless spell is over."

"My spirits are quite raised today. I must confide to you that at first I despaired of his recovery."

"Pooh," answered Julia, who refused to admit that she had had the same fear. "Has he asked for Catherine yet?"

"No, and I am persuaded he is aware she does not visit him."

"Perhaps he does not want her to see him ill."

Harriette nodded. "I am convinced that is true. And she in turn is too tenderhearted to bear the thought of her lover on the very edge of the River Styx."

"Yes!"

"I have been reading *The Old Manor House.*" Harriette changed the subject.

"Oh, I find Mrs. Smith's books so mysterious. That dreadful old mansion in the wind is horrifying. And when at the end. . . ."

"Pray, do not tell me. I can hardly wait to find out. In fact, I should read in here but would entirely forget to attend to Thomas. Catherine does not enjoy novels?"

"No. She is Gothic only insofar as it is fashionable. Beyond that she does not go." Julia laughed. "I cannot picture Catherine's appreciating what is dismal or savage in nature."

"Truly, it is difficult to see her outside the drawing room."

"She is happiest in London. I wonder, shall we enjoy the season?"

"I am convinced of it. That is, except for my sorrow."

"That is a great pity. Your brother must be brought round. But we must not think about it now. I wonder whom we shall meet and what the great parties will be like."

"Do you think we shall meet any of the more scandalous in town?"

"We must see that we do. I shall tell Grandmama. I should like to meet Lady Caroline Lamb. There is a most shocking story of her being carried into dinner hidden under the cover of a silver serving dish. When the lid was removed, there she was, completely . . ."

Harriette gave a little gasp. "You mean she . . . ? Without any . . . ?"

Julia nodded knowingly.

"How dreadful. But then what happened?"

"That is all I heard. One must imagine the rest."

Harriette's almond-shaped gray eyes were very wide. "How did you hear that?"

"My grandmama."

"I am sure Miss Marmion would never tell me on-dits if she knew of any. Although how either of us can hear news off in the country as we are is quite beyond me. Do you know any other stories?"

"Most of what I know is shocking."

"Indeed. But one must learn to face the world."

"Quite true. Well, I have heard there are those who have a *ménage à trois*."

"What is that?"

"Why a sort of three-way love affair, I think."

"How extraordinary. You do know some wonderfully shockings things. I cannot think what Miss Marmion would say."

"You had better not tell her."

"No indeed. Look, Thomas looks so peaceful now. There is even a faint smile on his face."

Julia went to the bed. "He is breathing quite evenly. I am sure he will now recover rapidly."

CHAPTER
SIX

It was time to practice on Norval. Doctor Linse had left for Vienna soon after the accident. He had not taken leave of Julia properly but had instead sent a message via Norval that he hoped to see her during the London season if good luck should see his return to England. He had managed to see Catherine and to wish her a farewell. Julia was relieved he was gone, for now she was free to get to work.

"Norval," she said as she walked with him one morning in the garden, "let us sit here in the summerhouse." Summer flowers opened to a lazy sun, and bees droned at their work.

Norval, ever courteous, led Julia into the latticeworked gazebo. As always, his dress was impeccable, the first stare of fashion. His suits were from Weston's; his hats, from Lock's; and his boots, from Hoby's. Today he looked the pink of *haut ton* with a *trône d'a-mour* knot to his necktie, a starched collar that kept his chin unusually high, dove-gray pantaloons, and a bottle-green jacket with eyepatch to match. As he was wont to hold his quizzing glass to his "good" eye, it was difficult to see what his face actually looked like. Julia decided that if eyes were the windows of the soul, Norval kept his well-shuttered.

"Norval, I think we should have a talk." Julia sat down and indicated that he was to take a place beside her.

"Yes, Mother agrees." He did as he was bid.

"Not that, Norval. Something quite different."

"Mother will be disappointed."

"I think it would be very nice if I should mesmerize you."

"Mesmerize? What made you think of that? Don't like that idea by half. Let's change the subject."

"Pray, Norval, do not get excited." She was using the well-modulated voice she had spent hours achieving. "Doctor Linse was not your friend. He mesmerized you and told you that you would forget the entire experience."

"Good for him. Want to forget. Nasty business, playing with the mind."

"You do not understand. He has already done so. You were a student of his in Vienna. I want to help you regain your knowledge of animal magnetism."

"What's the matter with your voice? Sounds decidedly odd. You never sounded like that before."

"Now, Norval, do pay attention to me."

"Not if you keep sounding like that. And why are

you staring at me? Maybe I ought to call the Marchioness."

"Norval, don't you understand? I want to help you."

"Seems to me you're the one who needs help. I came here feeling my best, and you try to make me believe something's the matter. You sound cocklebrained if you want my opinion."

"Don't be idiotish, Norval. Just do what I say. You are very relaxed now. Your eyes are becoming heavy."

"Relaxed? I most certainly am not relaxed. You feed me this skimble-skamble and tell me to relax."

"Norval, you make me furious."

"There. Now you sound more like yourself." He gazed at her through his quizzing glass. "This is all a hum, what?"

"Norval, you are a dolt, you are a pea-goose, you are a noddy."

"Now see here. What have I done?"

"You are caper-witted, addlebrained."

"I can see you're in no mood for our talk this morning, Julia. Don't know that I want to have it if you're going to keep this up." He stood, gave an exquisite bow, and walked toward home.

Julia, never one to be discouraged, walked back to the house. What a poor sport Norval had become. The Marchioness was right. He was too cossetted by his mother.

She found Thomas awake and propped up in a chair and Harriette with him. "Only two hours left to go," she reminded them proudly as though she had set the time for the bandages to be removed.

"How can we wait?" Harriette could not sit still but kept moving about the room on one pretense or another.

"Do be still, Harriette. You are making my head spin." The Duke laughed.

"She's right, Thomas. I cannot bear the tension."

"I am very grateful for your concern, Julia, and for your excellent nursing. But I expect that after these tedious weeks, you will be happy to see us on our way."

"How can you say that, Thomas? And you are not completely well, you know. You must remain with us a spell yet."

"I am glad I'm wanted, but I do feel guilty."

"Guilty?" The Marchioness poked her head in the door. "Ah, Stanfield, feeling fit are you? What about a game of cards to while away the time until Doctor Hugo arrives?"

"I fear Harriette could not keep up with this company, Marchioness."

"Nonsense. We've had a few games of an evening. Harriette?"

"I should love to, Marchioness."

"Good. Let's play at loo."

No sooner than this was decided, Witherspoon introduced a loo table into the chamber. He arranged the round table in front of his master's seat and placed three chairs for the others. He then produced a fresh pack of cards.

As the Marchioness shuffled, Thomas asked his sister if she would like the rules explained before beginning. "She has not a head for cards," he explained.

"Indeed," said the Marchioness, spreading the cards so the players could draw for dealer. But that was all she said. The two girls were unusually silent. Julia drew high card and dealt.

"Do you agree to eighteen-penny loo with the loo limited to half a guinea?" asked the Marchioness.

"Agreed," said the Duke, smiling. "Though if I am to pay for Harriette as well, I perceive I shall lose quite a little."

Harriette shook her head, holding up her reticule. "I shall pay my own debts, Thomas."

"I cannot think where you got the money."

"It doesn't signify."

The Duke was the first looed and had to pay his sum into the pool. "Harriette, I should not think to see you so pleased to watch me looed."

Harriette merely smiled.

It soon became apparent that Harriette was no novice to the game. Shortly before Doctor Hugo was to appear, Harriette had won a neat sum.

"I cannot think where you learned to play like that, Harriette." The Duke paused. "Or can I? Have you two been teaching her?"

"Promised you I'd teach her what she needed to learn, Stanfield."

"But, Marchioness, I perceived you to mean her studies."

"Studies? The child does little else but studies at home. Needed to know other things."

"What other things, pray?" asked the Duke, helplessly. The two girls broke out in peals of laughter.

"All the card games," gasped Julia.

"Has a good seat on a horse now, and light hands," added the Marchioness.

"And the Colonel has taught me to play at billiards," Harriette went on.

"You mean you two haven't taught her to shoot?"

"Oh, no," said Julia innocently. "Norval is a tolerably good shot, so he gave those lessons."

"And when have you done all this, pray?"

"While Witherspoon cared for you."

"Couldn't let your sister get ill tending a sickroom," said the Marchioness. "I held it my duty to see she had plenty of exercise and entertainment between sessions with you."

"I am much obliged, Marchioness, I think."

The girls laughed again until he was forced to join them.

"You'll have to admit, Stanfield, the girl is blooming. Pale little thing when I brought her here. Can't think what you're doing sticking her away in the country with nobody."

"But she has a staff of servants and an excellent governess."

"A wretched bore of a governess. I can't imagine that *you* spend time in Miss Marmion's company." Thomas colored a little as the remark struck home. "Come along, girls. Let's give the Duke a moment alone before the doctor arrives."

"But, Grandmama."

"Come along, both of you. That's better." She ushered them out.

When they had gone, the Duke gave Witherspoon a

penetrating look. "I was aware of the expression on your usually expressionless face while my sister was winning my money."

"Yes, Your Grace."

"I am persuaded you were decidedly pleased."

"Yes, Your Grace."

"Damn it, Witherspoon, are you loyal to me or are you not?"

"Most loyal to you, Your Grace."

"I'd like to know how," he grumbled.

"In showing appreciation of your sister's advancement in her studies, I am showing the greatest possible loyalty to your family."

"Advancement in her studies! What are they doing to my sweet little sister?"

"As the Marchioness remarked, Your Grace, she is 'blossoming.'"

"I have also perceived that anytime Miss Julia Hartman beats me at casino there is a decided gleam in your eye. I have discovered a serpent in our midst."

"Surely not I, Your Grace." Witherspoon's lips twitched. "As you are aware, I usually do not favor members of the female sex."

"That has been our policy, until lately."

"Might I say that you, Your Grace, were the first to change course."

"I did not change anything. I merely attended to my duty."

"Precisely so. And I do the same. But I find in attending to my duty that I have developed a decided partiality for Miss Julia as well as for Miss Harriette."

"That is exactly what I am accusing you of."

"Then, Your Grace, I stand before you guilty as charged."

"Humph!" ejaculated the Duke.

"That, Your Grace, is precisely what the Marchioness would say. Now I shall see if Doctor Hugo has arrived to remove the dressings."

Doctor Hugo was soon ushered in. While Julia, Harriette, and the Marchioness waited impatiently outside, the bandages were removed. At last the doctor appeared, looking rather grave. "You may come in now."

"Is it not remarkable how well His Grace looks?" said Witherspoon, with a warning glance from where he stood behind the Duke's chair.

"Remarkable." The Marchioness, smiling broadly, went to the Duke and shook his hand. "Congratulations, Stanfield, on doing so well."

"You think it is not too bad, then?" he asked hesitantly, a questioning look in his eyes.

"Bad? What kind of fiddle-faddle is that? A little scar. Go away in time. You've done well." She patted his cheek.

"You look very distinguished," said Julia, smiling. "Does he not, Harriette?"

"It is most romantic, Thomas. I am so pleased at how fine you look."

"Are you? You all relieve me considerably. Witherspoon, why can you not locate a glass somewhere, so I can judge for myself? And where is Catherine?"

"She is in the Pink Saloon waiting to hear. We said we should let her know," said Julia.

"I shall go directly, Your Grace." Witherspoon left hurriedly.

"The glass, Witherspoon. He doesn't hear. Could I trouble you for one, My Lady? There was one when I arrived, but Witherspoon removed it after the accident. Now he says it has disappeared."

"I collect he was searching for one, Stanfield. Thought the man was getting vain. Never dreamt you wanted it. I'll see one is brought in."

"Thank you, Marchioness. I began to think he feared a decided disfigurement."

"Nothing of the sort. Servants have been careless lately."

Soon Witherspoon entered. "Miss Catherine Hartman, Your Grace." Slowly he stood back to admit her.

"You took your time, Witherspoon. Catherine, how good to see you now that I am free of the wretched bandages. Catherine?"

She could say nothing; and despite Witherspoon's earlier admonishments, she merely stared. Not one word of what he had coached her to say remained in her head.

The Duke's face took on the look of horror in Catherine's. She ran from the room.

"A glass," he bellowed in an agony of pain, "bring me a glass!"

The Marchioness nodded to Witherspoon. He produced a small one from the dressing room bureau and reluctantly handed it to his master. The others stood, transfixed. Tears streamed down the girls' faces as he examined his reflection.

"Oh, my God!" He instinctively covered his face with his hands, letting the mirror slip. The only sound in the room was the shattering of the glass.

CHAPTER
SEVEN

"I am sorry, Miss Julia," said Witherspoon, truly apologetic. "He will see no one."

"But it has been three days."

"Three very long days, Miss Julia." He sighed.

"And you are too tired, Witherspoon. It is not fair to you."

"It cannot be helped."

"Indeed, everything can be helped. I shall see him."

"No, miss. He has given orders."

"Stuff and nonsense. Grandmama says this has gone on long enough."

"I quite agree with the Marchioness, but I cannot go against His Grace. He says we were all in league to bamboozle him, that we can none of us be trusted again."

"Does he! Well, he needn't trust us, but he is going

to have to put up with us. He is being very cruel not to see poor Harriette."

"Yes, miss. Is she feeling better?"

"She is fine. What is the Duke doing at the moment?"

"Staring out the window, I fear."

"Just as we suspected. I am determined to go in."

"I cannot allow it, Miss Julia."

"Stand aside, Witherspoon." She drew a pistol from the folds of her skirt.

He stepped back, stunned. "Surely you would not point a pistol at me, Miss Julia."

Her eyes twinkled. "No, my dear Witherspoon, you are very good to us all. But now you cannot refuse to admit me. And no blame can fall on you."

With what actually looked like a smile, Witherspoon opened the door and announced her.

"How dare you, Witherspoon? Crossing me again are you?"

"He has no choice, Thomas." Julia brandished her weapon.

"What, you pull a pistol on my manservant? And how dare you enter against my wishes?"

"Thomas, this will not do. You are in one wing of the house, sulking. Catherine is in another wing of the house, sulking. You must pull yourself together."

"Look at me. Why do you not shrink in terror as did your sister? I am hideous, a monster." He walked over to her, took her by the shoulders, and shook her. "Are you not afraid?"

"No. *You* are."

"*I?*"

"You are afraid people like you only for your good looks. You are afraid to see if they can like you for yourself."

"Do not be absurd. If I fear anything, it is to make people shudder. Can you imagine what it is like to have someone turn away from you, repulsed by the sight?"

"No, and I sympathize. But no one who loves you could ever be repulsed by you."

"Your sister is going to marry me, and she cannot look on me. Of course, now she must cry off."

"Depend upon it, she will not."

"But she must. I cannot."

"Then you must both start learning to live with a scar."

"You say that as if it were nothing at all."

"It is not what you make it."

"Oh, no? You and my foolish sister seem to see my disfigurement as something romantic, something out of a novel."

"It is decidedly *not* novel material, Thomas. Heroes in novels are neither vain nor are they unkind. I shall leave you to Witherspoon, but the poor man is sadly in need of rest and should certainly not be employed as watchdog. It was only Harriette and I who wished to see you, and we shall stay away." She swept from the room.

Harriette met her in the hall. "What happened?"

"Shh. Come along." Julia led her to the Marchioness' room, where the old lady sat playing solitaire.

"And was it very nasty, child?" she asked without looking up.

"Tolerably so. Just as you said, he was furious at first about the pistol."

"Then tried to justify his self-pity, did he?"

"That's right."

"Then made you out to be some kind of nincompoop for accepting his scar?"

"Just like that, Grandmama. I am so glad you warned me, or he would have hurt me deeply."

"He's lashing out, child. Take no notice. You *did* let him know he hurt your feelings?"

"Oh, yes. I was wonderful. Harriette, I wish you could have been there. He said we were both foolish and romantic, and I told him he was unkind and we should not return."

"How did he look when you said that?" The Marchioness added a card to her hearts.

"Very startled."

"Good. Just so."

"Dear me," sighed Harriette. "Do you really think this will help?"

"Naturally," snapped the Marchioness. "He feels guilty now. Get him off self-pity for a time."

"I forgot to say I added Witherspoon to the guilt."

"Excellent. Wouldn't have thought of that myself." This was high praise, and Julia beamed.

"But what do we do now?" wondered Harriette.

"We wait," said the Marchioness. "We wait. He is already quite bored or he wouldn't have been so willing to quarrel. You two have spoiled him to death, and that is not easy to give up. He'll send for you."

"But he is proud."

"Guilt and boredom can work wonders. And unless

110

I sadly misjudge Witherspoon, he is adding a little fuel to the fire we have kindled."

"I am so relieved. What should we do without you, Marchioness?"

"I expect you'd get on famously. Now, why not go into the garden for some fresh air. I should not be readily available if I was sent for." She looked up and winked. "I should be sent for more than once."

The Colonel, Mrs. Hartman, and Catherine were in the sitting room off Catherine's bedchamber. "My dear," admonished Catherine's mother, dabbing at her eyes with a lace handkerchief, "you really must see him."

"This won't do, you know," added the Colonel. "Hang it all, you're engaged to the man."

"Can you think I do not know that?" Catherine fanned herself. Her eyes were swollen. "I cannot face him now."

"Can't see why not." The Colonel lit a cigar.

"I have tried to explain. I was so horrified. You cannot imagine. I did not even have the good manners to cover up what I felt. I certainly cannot now say he looks fine."

"I am told the other girls said so," said Mrs. Hartman meekly. "I do not know what we are to do."

"Calm yourself, my dear." The Colonel blew smoke rings and watched them disappear.

"It is all very well for the other two," said Catherine. "Harriette is his sister, and Julia does not have to marry him."

"I suppose Catherine could cry off, Colonel, but I

should hate to think that necessary. It is such a perfect match, and with a Duke."

"Hate to see it myself, don't you know, but she can't marry a man she don't want to look at. I think she should cry off. Jolly awkward otherwise."

"Do you suppose you could learn to look at him, Catherine dear? Remembering the suitability of the match, of course."

"I must. I shall not cry off."

"Then you must see him," said the Colonel.

"Dear me. What is to be done, Colonel?"

"Can't think why you won't cry off, Catherine."

"Do you not see how guilty I am that this has happened? How can I desert him after being the cause of his disfigurement?"

"Come, daughter, he don't blame you. If that's why you'll marry him, I say it is more honorable to give it up."

"I cannot forgive myself," wailed Catherine.

"What is to be done? What is to be done?" sighed Mrs. Hartman. "Life used to be much less complicated, I am sure. You know," she brightened, "the dear man has so many estates, perhaps you could contrive not to see him so very often." This brought a fresh wail from Catherine, so her mother produced the vinaigrette. "Young people are not the same today. I cannot think what is happening to the world."

"Now, Clarissa, calm yourself," said the Colonel. "The only answer is for Catherine to see him, get used to his looks if she can, and if she cannot, to cry off. That, my girl, is what you will do."

"But, Papa. . . ."

"We've talked enough to no advantage. You'll see him. He is, after all, a guest in this house. Whoever heard of refusing to see a guest? Isn't done."

"What if," sniffled Catherine, "he won't see me?"

"You must make the first effort."

"All right, Papa. I see there is no help for it."

"Good girl."

Julia and Harriette, in pastel frocks, sat in the summerhouse. It was a fine day, and rain clouds that had threatened to mar a spell of warm weather had drifted away in the night.

"To think he has not yet sent for us. Is the Marchioness ever wrong?"

"Never. We must be patient."

"But she suggested we should not go to him the first time he requests it."

"We shan't. We shall make him come to us."

"Your grandmama did not say that."

"One must learn to improvise."

"I suppose you are right. But what exactly is your improvisation?"

"I collect you will see shortly. Here is Witherspoon with our summons."

"How clever of him to find us here."

"Not at all. When one is waiting for a summons, one makes sure she can be found."

"Then we are not here by accident?"

"Certainly not. The Marchioness does not believe much in chance."

"Young ladies," Witherspoon stood at the gazebo steps, "my master sends me to summon you."

"I see, Witherspoon," said Julia, casually. "Could you relate his message to us?"

"I believe I can. His Grace said, 'Witherspoon, you had better tell those two young scamps to come up here.'"

"So that is the message. I thought it might be in those terms." Julia walked about the gazebo, fanning herself with an ivory fan. "It is, of course, obvious to you, Witherspoon, that we are busy at the moment and cannot possibly attend the Duke."

"Perfectly obvious, Miss Julia. And is that the message I am to take?"

"Partly. The Duke may attend us here if he wishes."

Harriette gasped. "But he has not left his room. He will not."

"That is our message, Witherspoon. We shall be happy to receive him and give him a few moments of our time if he chooses to come to the summerhouse."

"Very good, miss." Witherspoon's eyes twinkled as he left to convey his message.

"Oh, Julia, he will be furious. And he will never come."

"Well, he cannot sit in that room forever. I am convinced that Grandmama is right. He is very bored indeed, and anything can be endured but boredom."

"He will never admit it."

"No. But he will find some excuse to come down. I expect he will say he is worried about you."

"Here you are, Julia." Norval entered the summerhouse, looking unexceptionable in pantaloons of York tan, and celestial blue coat and eye patch. "A fellow can't ever find you. You might leave word with the servants where you are. Harriette."

"Hello, Norval," said Julia.

"Hello, Lord Devon," answered Harriette, politely. "Will you join us?"

"Already have, thank you. Warm day, what? Perhaps you ladies would care to take a stroll?"

"Not now, Norval."

"What's wrong with now? You're not in another mood are you, Julia?"

"I cannot think that I have ever been in a mood."

"Julia does not have moods, Lord Devon."

"Don't tell me. I grew up with her. Never knew such a one for moods. Hard to please." Norval settled himself on a gazebo bench. "I suppose we can chat here."

"You must not let us detain you, Norval," said Julia, icily.

"Glad to keep you company. I say, Harriette, you're getting to be as fidgety as Julia. Won't do, once you come out. Supposed to have some sort of address. Ladies at Almack's won't like fidgeting. Can't say the men will line up to dance with either of you when you both look ready to come down with a fit of the vapors. Must be the air. Mother claims it isn't what it should be this summer. Ought to go inside. Can't see why you're sitting here anyway."

"Do be still, Norval," snapped Julia.

"Now what have I done? A fellow's got to think mighty fast not to offend you, Julia. Here I am, chatting pleasantly, and you go and get offended again."

"Look, Julia, there he is."

"There who is? Oh, your brother. Can't think what's so special about seeing your brother. Should be used to him by now. Probably coming to ask what the deuce you're sitting here for. I should think, Harriette, you'd want another lesson with the pistols. You're a fair shot now but could be much better."

"She's good enough for all practical purposes, Norval."

"See here. She's my pupil. I'll be the one to say how well she shoots and if there's to be more lessons."

"That's very kind of you, Norval."

"Not at all, Harriette. I say, Stanfield, do join us. Pleasant day, what?"

The Duke, a scowl on his face, came up the gazebo steps. "What are you two doing here?"

"Exactly what I asked them. Got some notion they want to sit here. Can't think why."

"And you had the effrontery to send for me."

"Sent for you, did they? Didn't send for me. I had a devilish time finding them. You might have let me know, Julia, especially if you're sending for people. Haven't sent for any more have you? Didn't expect a crowd."

Julia glared at him. "There's to be no crowd, Norval."

"I should think not," grumbled the Duke. "Harriette, how can you let me worry about you like this? You fail to come to my room. I don't know what has become of you. You force me to come in search of you."

"I'm the one who had to search!" exclaimed Norval. "You was sent for. Rum thing to do, Julia. Sending for people to come here when there's nothing to do once they arrive. I say, Stanfield, let's leave these two to sit here while we have some shooting, what?"

"Shooting? You talk of shooting?"

"Well, I'd sooner get to it than talk about it."

"Now?"

"Don't tell me you want to sit in the summerhouse, 'cause I assure you, there's nothing to do here."

"Look at me. Just look at me."

"Keep repeating yourself, Stanfield. What am I supposed to look at?"

"I haven't yet seen the look of horror creep over your features."

"I should think not. Julia, are you going to tell me something to upset me? Out with it. But I won't show no horror, you can depend upon it."

"Look at me."

"You said that, old fellow. Let me get my quizzing glass to my eye. Hmm. Yes. I see what you mean. Should have had your coat made at Weston's. Shoulder line's a hair's breadth off. Don't think most would notice, though. Put your mind at rest."

"My face, you dolt. My face."

"Now don't *you* go insulting me. No cause. What about your face?"

"Aren't you thoroughly repulsed by the scar?"

"Can't say I'd given it any thought." He looked long and hard through his quizzing glass. "Puts me in mind of my last duel. That's nothing compared to what I

117

could do to you. Got off lucky, what?" He surveyed the Duke again. "Those shoulders won't quite do. A new coat's the answer. But never mind for now. Get your pistols, and I'll meet you by the stables in a few minutes."

The Duke, looking a little perplexed, walked back for his pistols.

"Norval," said Julia when Thomas had gone. "I could kiss you. I shall kiss you." She stood on tiptoe and kissed him on the cheek.

"Julia, are you sure you're all right?"

Harriette kissed him as well, and he left the summerhouse muttering something about moods and bad air and being glad that the London season would soon begin.

CHAPTER
EIGHT

"I think it is quite nice that Catherine sees the Duke for an hour each day." Mrs. Hartman spooned pudding onto her plate.

"But she still acts repulsed by him," Julia complained.

"You cannot blame me," insisted Catherine. "I do the best I can." Her eyes filled with tears.

"I'm sure you do," comforted the Colonel.

The Marchioness said nothing.

"Yet I cannot think why he does not join us for meals," Mrs. Hartman continued. "Julia, you and Harriette have had almost no meals with the family lately. That poor little sister, so devoted. I expect he will go home soon."

"Oh, he must not go yet!" exclaimed Julia.

"But he is fit," said Mrs. Hartman. "At least as fit as ever he will be, dear boy."

"But he must get to know us better."

"I cannot imagine how, if he stays in that room. Oh dear, it is all so unfortunate. Why, I wonder, Colonel, do such unfortunate things happen to me?"

"Don't trouble yourself, Clarissa, my dear. As Bentham says, 'There must be a balance between pleasure and pain.'"

"To be sure, Colonel."

"Why when one thinks of the world today and the feature of diminishing utility . . ."

"I," announced the Marchioness, rising and interrupting him, "shall go to my room. Julia, will you attend an old lady?"

"To be sure, Grandmama."

"No cards, Grandmother?" asked Catherine in surprise.

"Not tonight. I am indisposed."

"Perhaps it was the quail or the truffles. You had such a good dinner, as always, Mother. And you are never ill."

"I am when it suits me to be. Come along, Julia, and help me to my room." She marched out, her granddaughter in attendance.

"I have a plan," said the old lady as they entered her chamber. "This won't do at all, you know, not as it's going."

"You are right, Grandmama. Everything seems to be at a standstill."

"So it is up to us to move things along. Look here." She held out a small jar to Julia. "Well, take it, child."

Julia accepted it, wonderingly. "What can it be?"

"Magic, child. Magic. When all else fails, try magic."

Julia opened the lid and touched her forefinger to a thick cream. "For the scar?"

"The imbecile doctors never know what to do. The Marquess used this once after being wounded in battle. It softens the skin so that the scar will not be so noticeable. If you can get him to believe in the cream, it may do wonders."

"How can that be?"

"Believing in anything is half the battle, child. If he believes in the cream, he will think it is working, and who knows what wonders his body may perform?"

"Grandmama, I fear it is just an ordinary cream, after all."

"Then it will be. You must help to put the magic in it."

Julia's eyes lit up. "I think I see. We shall try it."

"Of course, we'll try it. Run along now."

Julia gave her grandmother a hug. "You think of everything."

"Humph. Somebody's got to. Foolish household. Nobody keeps his head on his shoulders. You stay sensible, child, you hear? There's got to be one sensible person in every family. All nitwits." She settled herself on the bed with a new novel by Monk Lewis.

Julia skipped down the dark hall and knocked cautiously at the Duke's bedchamber door. Her ankle-length dress with vandyked falling collar was trimmed with pink ribbons. She had hit upon the idea that color was all important in raising the Duke's spirits and had decided with Harriette to wear only pink or yellow whenever possible. A pale blue was permissible but nothing dark, no green, and no scarlet whatsoever because that might remind him of the accident. Several of their dresses had been sent to the seamstress to be re-embroidered.

"Come in," said a stern voice. Julia smoothed her skirt, then peered inside to find the Duke alone.

"I have a surprise for you," she announced proudly.

"My dear girl, everything you do surprises me."

"But this will astonish you."

"I doubt that I am up to being astonished." He lolled in an easy chair and stared out the window, a disinterested look on his virile face. Julia noticed that beneath his puce dressing gown of velvet, he wore a white necktie with an impeccable knot. He looked at her with his dark, ironic eyes, and she found it hard to keep from trembling slightly. "Here." She thrust the jar at him.

He took it, continuing to gaze at her. "And what is this, pray tell?"

"Magic."

"Indeed." He opened the lid as Julia had done. "I perceive it is a cream of some sort. Am I to understand that I am to apply it to my scar which will then disappear like magic?"

"Not so simple as that," she answered, drawing up a chair beside him. "It will soften the skin so that the scar will fade somewhat."

"Somewhat!" he repeated bitterly.

"Oh, we shouldn't want it to fade entirely. It is such a distinguishing mark."

"But you do want it to fade somewhat?"

"*I* do not, Thomas. *You* do, and I am trying to help you."

"Then do not tempt me with magic nonsense."

"It is not nonsense. The Marchioness has sent it because it did wonders for the Marquess when he was wounded."

"She thinks it will help?"

"She *knows* it will help."

"I suppose it cannot hurt to humor the old lady."

"See here, if my grandmama says it will work, it will work. You need not humor her." Julia snatched the jar back.

"Not so hasty, please. I did not mean to insult your grandmother. I am quite indebted to her. Forgive me for being so bad tempered."

"I understand," said Julia, rising and walking toward the door.

"And will you not leave me the cream?"

"Only if you insist, for I know Norval would dearly love to have it. He manages to get into at least one scrape a season and is sure to be scarred himself eventually."

"By all means I should like it."

"I shall put it on the bureau, then, and you must use it three times a day, upon awaking, at noon, and before retiring."

"I shall use your magic, you little witch, and it had better make me more acceptable to your sister. And do not pout. I thought you wanted me to use it."

"I want you to be happy, Thomas."

"If it works, I shall be the happiest man alive, and you will celebrate as maid-of-honor at your sister's wedding. Now come sit down and read me a little poetry."

"I think Harriette has been looking for me. I shall attend you later." She turned and slipped from the room before he could see two large tears escape from her eyes and wend their way down her cheeks.

"Just think, the London season is almost upon us!" exclaimed Julia as she sat with Thomas and Harriette in his chamber. "I cannot wait to visit Gunther's in Berkeley Square. Grandmama says our cook gets all his pastries there, and Gunther sells fruit ices from Greenland."

"Surely they would melt," objected Harriette.

"No. As soon as they arrive, blocks of ice are buried under the cellars where they are stored. Catherine says she prefers the ices to other delicacies."

"I think I shall, too."

The Duke made no comment. He seemed to want them with him but did not always join in the conversation. Julia would sometimes look up to see him watching her, an expression she could not understand on his face.

"Of course, I should most like to visit the gaming clubs," Julia went on. "I can see myself gambling at Boodle's or Brooks's or White's. I hear that there is so much money exchanging hands at White's that Raggett, the proprietor, sends all the servants away and sweeps up the carpets himself to discover all the gold."

"Do you play there, Thomas?" asked Harriette, wide-eyed.

"Certainly." He laughed. "And do not think that story is idle gossip. If you knew Raggett, you would be convinced of its veracity."

"How fortunate men are," sighed Julia.

They could hear Witherspoon in the dressing room, packing for the journey to the Duke's favorite country estate. Thomas and Harriette would return home until the season would commence, when they would all meet in London. Julia decided this would be her last chance to broach the subject of Lord Effly before then, and who knew what plans could be agreed upon in the meantime? Harriette sat looking so very pensive that Julia knew Thomas must now be swayed.

"Thomas," she began in her usual abrupt way that some said was rather similar to that of the Marchioness, "I think it a shame that each time the season is mentioned, Harriette becomes downcast."

"If my sister is given to moods, she will have to learn to control them."

"I am not given to moods, Thomas."

"You look to be in one at the moment."

"And why would she not be? She must lie awake nights imagining marrying that odious Lord Effly; and to think, she has not even had the chance to meet another."

"Odious, you say? Odious? He is one of my best friends."

"Do not fly into a miff. It is clear to see that he is not Harriette's best friend. Surely, you cannot want your own sister to marry one on whom she does not bestow her affections?"

"Do not speak in such a skittier-witted fashion. He

125

is a fine fellow and the match is perfect. One cannot ask for more."

"Love, Thomas, love. One can ask for that."

"My girl, your excessive sympathy is quite moving. I can only tell you that it is misplaced. My sister is in a very fortunate circumstance. If she chooses to act as if she is in a Cheltenham tragedy, I cannot be to blame." Suddenly the injured party, he glanced out the window, then turned back abruptly. "I wish you will not encourage her in this matter. I collect she was quite resigned to this marriage until under your influence."

Harriett looked dismayed. "Thomas, that is not true. You know that it is not. Julia has changed my thinking on the matter not at all."

"I find that hard to believe, as she seems to have changed almost everyone's thinking on every matter."

Julia arose and stood by the window. "You are not, I hope, suggesting that I meddle."

"I should never had considered such an idea." The Duke watched her, a faint smile on his lips.

"An interest in life, Thomas. That is what I take, an interest in life. *You,* I have noticed, have a quite different philosophy."

"My God, right on target. I should take you to Manton's gallery for some shooting. You would put all the Corinthians to shame."

"Please, do not quarrel on my account."

"What do you expect, Harriette, when you air your complaints to the world at large?"

"I am not the world at large, Thomas."

"Humph. You have taught me to exaggerate."

"I should have preferred to teach you something else."

"I think Effly quite a handsome fellow," he mused. "That is more than can be said of me at present."

"But looks mean nothing."

"You think not? I recall vividly the comments made about how well your sister and I looked together. You notice I say, 'looked.' Past tense. Nevermore. Yes, this talk reminds me of my own purpose—to marry a lovely girl, who is repulsed by my appearance."

"She comes to see you each day, Thomas," objected Julia. "I am convinced you are wrong."

"Are you? She grows more beautiful and more quiet each day. Still, it is an excellent match. At least she will bring beauty to the marriage if I cannot. Come to think, all eyes will be on her, so they may not even notice my face. Perhaps it is the best possible match for us both. Julia, I am grateful you brought the subject up. You see, Harriette, the proper match is the thing. Then you go about, as I have done, making the very best of the situation. You must learn how to approach life optimistically as you see me do. When you know Effly better, you will find him a very agreeable man. Julia, you have cheered us both immensely."

CHAPTER
NINE

"I don't know why I let you bamboozle me into coming to London for the season," complained the Colonel as the Marchioness' blue and gold barouche drew to a stop in Grosvenor Square. The house was a favorite of both the Marchioness and Julia. It had a melancholy exterior, the sort one might expect from a castle, a dark-paneled cedar saloon, and dusky hallways; in short, every aspect to titillate the imagination. The Colonel had been allowed to touch nothing here, and the antiquated kitchen, used by Filmore, the chef, was off bounds for everyone, including the Marchioness. Filmore adored London, refused to go to the country out of season, collected an unreasonable salary, and was said to be second only to the famous Ude (though some whispered that the Regent had once said that Filmore surpassed Ude).

"I see what you mean, Father. This house dampens my spirits," said Catherine, whose spirits had appeared dampened for some time.

Mrs. Hartman fanned herslf and sniffed at her vinaigrette. "This journey never fails to exhaust me."

"Don't be cocklebrained, daughter. It's good for you to get some air. There's nothing like travel to make you feel exhilarated." However, Julia and the Marchioness appeared to be the only two who had reaped that benefit. The family alighted, tho large doors were opened, and the stay for another season commenced.

"He ain't pleased, I can tell you," said the Marchioness as the family lunched in the dining hall.

"But he must let her come, Grandmama."

"I for one, think we should not meddle in the Duke's household," said Catherine, picking daintily at her food.

"We do not want to offend him," ventured Mrs. Hartman.

"It is about time somebody did meddle," snorted the Marchioness. "That poor child. Is she supposed to be under the influence of that dreadful Miss Markion all season?"

"Miss Marmion, Grandmama."

"Don't correct me, child. Whatever the woman calls herself, she's a bore. Who's to escort Harriette to the parties? Not that dreadful Aunt Pinksnob, I should hope."

"It is Pentsnub, Grandmama."

"No matter what way she pronounces it, she's a

bore as well. Never liked the woman. Never shall."

"Mother, you really must try."

"Shan't try. I'm much too old to do anything but please myself."

"Do see that Harriette comes to stay, Grandmama."

"*À mon avis*, Grandmother," sighed Catherine, "Julia should not always have her own way."

"Indeed not," snapped the Marchioness with a sniff, "but I shall have mine. I didn't live this long to cater to others, especially since I always know what's best." She winked at Julia.

"It is an embarrassment for me," said Catherine, "but if you persist in pestering the Duke, *il n'y a rien à faire.*"

"You're quite right," said the Colonel, laughing. "There is no help for it. I think Harriette is a charming girl and should join our livelier household."

All looked up as the doors opened and Benton showed in Lord Devon, so frequent a visitor that he entered at any hour.

"Will you have a glass of wine, Norval dear?" asked Mrs. Hartman. One was brought immediately as he seated himself near Julia.

"All rather serious, what? Should see the pair of grays I bought at Tattersell's today. That would liven your spirits."

"Oh, there are lively spirits here, my lad." The Colonel indicated he would have more wine as well. "We were just discussing having Lord Stanfield's sister to stay."

"Jolly idea, that. Nice girl, Harriette. Very polite." He looked pointedly at Julia. "No moods."

"I am sure she never has moods," said Mrs. Hartman. "She has seemed very even to us. What makes you think, Norval, that she has moods?"

"I think she don't, ma'am."

"Then how strange of you to mention them. Dear me, I shouldn't like it if she has moods. I remember once, Colonel, when we were courting, thinking you had moods. It was the most amusing thing, children."

"Amusing!" grumbled the Colonel. "She let her hat fly into the lake, and I had to wade in after it. Then she said I was in a mood."

"You should have seen his face. Oh, how angry he was."

"Wouldn't have gone in if you hadn't been tossing it into the air."

"It was such a lovely day, and the wind was blowing, and the Colonel looked so ridiculous wading into the water. What fun we had when we were young."

"Sounds quite a lark," said Norval.

"*Revenons à nos moutons.* Is Harriette to come or is she not?"

"I decided that long ago, my girl," answered Catherine's grandmother. "Naturally, she'll come."

"But if Thomas persists in declining the invitation?"

"He won't decline again, you may be sure. We should hear any minute now that he'll be delighted to let his dear sister stay with us. Benton, is it not time for the afternoon mail?"

"Danvil is only now fetching it, My Lady."

The footman returned with several notes on a sterling salver and handed them to Her Ladyship. She shuffled quickly through the pile and pulled one out with satisfaction. "This should be it." She opened the missive, a look of triumph on her face. "How very good of you to request the pleasure of my dear sister's company. She will be delighted to stay with you. I send my deepest thanks for such kind hospitality."

"How very remarkable!" exclaimed Mrs. Hartman.

The Marchioness chuckled. "Not at all, Clarissa."

"Now we shall have quite a time," said Julia.

"Glad that's settled." The Colonel arose. "I'll be on my way to hear Fox speak. Can't think whom I admire most, Fox or Sheridan. Wonderful to hear a great orator, don't you know? Don't suppose you'd like to accompany me, Norval?"

"Me, sir? I should think not. Speeches ain't my cup of tea."

"I can't say I ever did know what your cup of tea is, Norval."

"I'll give that some thought, sir. Can't remember anyone ever asking me that. Interesting question, what?"

"I'll be off, then." The Colonel kissed his wife goodby.

"Grandmama, how did you do it?"

"I shan't give all my secrets away. I always keep a little magic for myself."

So Harriette came to stay, with admonishments from the Duke never to ask the cost of anything while shopping as it was bad form, never to be seen walking down St. James's Street or Bond Street in the morning unless accompanied by a maid, and to be seen there in the afternoon not at all under pain of being ostracized from polite society.

"My dear Stanfield," said the Marchioness, "we shall see that Harriette knows all the correct things to do."

"I had rather, Marchioness, that you would see she *does* the correct things."

"Just leave her to me, Stanfield."

"That is what I fear." The Duke shook his head in a bewildered fashion as he took his leave.

"I have a surprise for you," said the Marchioness when he was gone. "Look outside."

The girls ran to the window to see a smart curricle. A tiger held the horses. "That's so you can ride where you like."

"Marchioness, how exciting. But there is just room for two. Who shall drive us?"

"Julia, my dear. She is no mean hand with the ribbons. I expect you two will be the rage in Hyde Park."

"And we are to drive between five and six? That is what my brother said, I believe."

"You're to drive anytime, any place, or almost any place. Use your good judgment. That's why it was given to you. I suggest you don't always do what the fashionable are doing, or you won't stand out."

"But my brother said I was not to attract any undue attention by any deviation from what is most acceptable."

"Then you'll never attract anyone but Effly, my girl. Unless," and she smiled, "that is what you want?"

Both girls laughed. "Thank you, Grandmama." Julia kissed her.

"Don't go thanking me. Can't bear that sort of

thing. Well, go on. Get into your carriage. I understand it's one Stanfield has been admiring. I imagine he'll have quite a surprise to see you in it."

"What if he should mind, Marchioness?"

"Mind? We can't put his sister in anything but the best. Now run along, and don't be late for supper. Effly is joining us. It's time we looked him over and planned our campaign. Off with you."

The girls put on their bonnets and lightweight shawls and hurried out to the awaiting curricle. Julia took the whip, and away they rode at a rather daring clip, Julia driving the horses well up to their bits. "These two are sweet goers," she announced as she drove to an inch while rounding a corner.

The girls noticed that more than one pedestrian paused to watch their progress. Suddenly, Harriette grabbed Julia's arm, causing Julia to rein in the horses. "There." She pointed and looked very pale.

"I do not see anything to disturb us. Oh!" for she had just caught sight of the Duke, alighting from his barouche with another man. "They have looked this way. We must carry on." Julia had her horses step in a stately manner down the street. "We shall smile graciously as we pass and continue on our way."

It was not that easy. The Duke called to them, and they were forced, under pain of rudeness, to delay their progress. Although his scar had improved considerably with the cream, his temper had not. He stood scowling while the girls inwardly trembled. "Do I not recognize that carriage?" The girls did not answer. "Miss Hartman, may I present Lord Effly?"

Julia was too surprised to answer. She found the despised lover to be a personable looking gentleman, but as he talked, he seemed far stuffier than his years should have allowed.

"Young ladies," he commenced, "did you not know that the hour to ride out is five and the place, Hyde Park? Perhaps, Stanfield, we could drive them home in your barouche and send a tiger for the curricle. And imagine riding about without your tiger."

"But you must see, Lord Effly," said Julia demurely, "that there is room for only two. Did I have my tiger with me, you would not have had the good fortune to meet Harriette at this moment."

"I am shocked to see my soon to be affianced riding about town like a, like a, like a common woman."

Julia looked shocked. "Surely, Lord Effly, you do not compare your affianced with one of the Fashionable Impures, as I understand such ladies are called."

The Duke had to stifle a smile. "What Effly means, my dear young ladies, is that you do yourselves no credit by this behavior."

"Oh," sighed Julia, while Harriette merely peeped from her bonnet. "I am relieved to hear your meaning. For surely the Cyprians, as I prefer to call them, take their tigers everywhere. I have heard of none who is a good whip."

"Damn your impudence!"

"Duke?" Julia fluttered her eyelids slightly and opened her large violet eyes even wider. "Your meaning, sir? An oath before ladies and in public? We, your dear sister and I, are quite shocked. Are we not shocked, Harriette?"

"Oh, very, very shocked." Harriette, having looked

shocked from the start, had no need to change her expression.

"You have heard me say far worse than that, you little hypocrite."

"Indeed, do not remind us, sir. I am quite faint with the memory. Harriette, dear friend, do you have the smelling bottle?"

"N—no." stammered her friend.

"There is no help for it. I must then have a little hartshorn and water. We shall leave you now."

"See here," the Duke commenced, only to be interrupted by Lord Effly, who announced, "I will not allow Harriette to expose herself to the public eye in this way. Do you hear?"

"Dear sir," said Julia, "I hear nothing. My head simply reels with the vibrations of Duke Stanfield's unseemly ejaculation." She put her hand to her forehead. "Adieu, gentlemen. Let us hope when we meet again, it will be in happier circumstances. Oh, Harriette, I am so thankful Catherine could not hear this."

In a rather abrupt change, she cracked her whip, and the horses, already used to her command, obeyed instantaneously, leaving the two gentlemen in a rage at the curbside.

"Oh, Julia, he is so angry."

"I daresay." She laughed, and Harriette had to join in.

"But he can stop us from riding out."

"He will have to do it through my grandmama."

"Then I do feel easier."

"I see what you mean about Lord Effly. I do think

him good-looking with fine features. It is when he speaks that he damns himself. He is a colossal snob."

"But do you think the Marchioness will take to him?"

"Certainly not. She cannot bear a snob. She finds such a person terribly boring, and you know how she hates to be bored."

"I think you are right. I feel ever so much better."

"Yes. That was a happy meeting. I know better now how to deal with Lord Effly. But how nice if we could meet somebody you could truly admire."

"And you?"

Julia blushed and attended to her driving. Both girls were agog at the traffic of carriages and pedestrians, and the noise of the pedlars and street criers, the clatter of horses' hoofs and wheels. People seemed to be hurrying, each to a different destination, and no doubt each thought his own journey of major importance.

"You know your way around well," admired Harriette.

"I have studied. However, I have taken a few wrong turns which you did not notice. No matter. Here we finally are at Hookam's."

The girls alighted, motioning to a street boy to hold the horses. Then they entered to get what was first on their list: library books. "I doubt that we shall ever want to leave here. I have dreamed of visiting for ever so long," said Julia as they entered. "I, too," answered her companion.

The girls did finally leave with volumes by Jane Austen, Oliver Goldsmith, Charlotte Smith, Monk

Lewis, Mrs. Radcliffe, and Charles Robert Maturin, among others.

"Do you think we shall have enough to read?" asked Harriette, staggering under her load.

"No. We shall return as often as necessary. Just think of all we shall learn about life from these. And I do not doubt Grandmama will enjoy them."

They next stopped at the silk mercers in Mayfair, then at Clark & Debenham of Cavendish House, Wigmore Street, to pick out feathers for their bonnets. It was all so exciting that the girls soon found that the hour for driving in Hyde Park had almost passed.

"We must not miss this," insisted Julia, pulling Harriette away from artificial flowers meant to adorn wide-brimmed hats. "We must let it be known that we are in town. As Grandmama says, we shall have to attract some little attention."

"But we must be careful not to offend the ladies of Almack's."

"Pooh. We shall offend no one, only attract a few." She laughed. "Though that might offend your brother and Lord Effly."

"How I should like to offend Lord Effly. Only think, he has offended me for ever so long."

"Quite right." Julia pulled into the park. "Here we are at the arena. Remember, your only weapons are your smile and your eyes, which can be killing when used correctly."

"I shall observe you."

"You may, Harriette, but you must develop your own style. I am convinced of that. I have failed utterly attempting to use Catherine's. Oh, no! Here comes

Norval. How can we be charming with Norval about? Well, there's no help for it. Lord Devon," she smiled and bowed her head slightly as Norval rode up on his gray.

"Lord Devon! You've never called me that in your life. Tried to get you to ever so often. Now it seems very unfriendly. Afternoon, Harriette."

"Norval." She tried to nod as Julia had done.

"What's the matter with you two? Harriette, you're acting as strange as Julia."

"We are being charming, Norval," said Julia icily.

"Charming! Well, you ain't charmed me. Won't charm nobody if you go around bobbing your heads like puppets."

"I gave you a glance and a discreet nod, Norval, and Harriette did the same."

"So I noticed. Well, don't do it again is all I can say. You gave me more than one nod. I am certain you gave more than one nod. Looked like you had the blasted palsy."

"Norval, you become boring."

"You observe, I take no notice of your insults, Julia. The Marchioness told me to take no notice."

"You may take no notice of me at all, Norval."

"Wouldn't do that. I'll ride about with you."

"No, no, Norval. We shall not detain you."

"Glad to oblige. I intend to escort you both every afternoon."

"Every afternoon?" squeaked Harriette.

"Weather permitting. Let's go along this path."

"But we go this way, Norval." Julia indicated the path in the opposite direction.

"Glad to oblige." He swung his gray about.

So the three rode around the park during the appropriate hour, the girls nodding and smiling to those they recognized; and more than one young gentleman detained them and asked Lord Devon for an introduction.

"Look, in that *vis-à-vis*," whispered Julia so that Norval could not hear as they progressed along their way. "I am certain it is the courtesan known as the Mocking Bird. Grandmama says you can always pick out the Cyprians, for they have the finest carriages, the handsomest horses, the tallest footmen, and the most elaborate liveries of any of the *beau monde*. Look at the plumes in her hair. The gentlemen certainly are not making themselves scarce. And only notice, your brother and Lord Effly are among her admirers. So that is the sort they know, and we are to sit at home with needlework. Tra la, we shall tease them for this. They will not know we understand who she is."

In a few moments the Duke and Lord Effly caught sight of the curricle and rode over to pay their respects. "I shall never forgive you for having the curricle I had quite set my mind to," grumbled the Duke after greetings were said.

"But you are welcome to ride in it at any time," said Julia sweetly. "Do tell us who your lovely friend is in the *vis-à-vis*. We should love to meet her and perhaps invite her to nuncheon. Harriette does want to be gracious to all your friends."

"Indeed I do," said Harriette. "You must introduce us."

"No. She is no one you would like. Isn't it a fine day for an outing."

"I did observe," Julia smiled at Lord Effly, "that you, sir, seemed very much in the lady's favor. Is she some secret amour?"

"Nothing of the kind," sputtered his Lordship. "I do not know the, uh, the lady well. I have just met her at a few gatherings."

"What delightful gatherings they must be," said Harriette.

"And without your affianced? They must have been recent gatherings for the, uh, lady to remember you so well."

"You must take me to the next such fête," said Harriette, smiling.

"But we must go." Julia raised her whip. "I see that it is almost six, the close of the fashionable hour. Adieu, gentlemen. Lord Devon, pray escort us home."

They left the two gentlemen, both of whom looked rather red in the face. Norval rode with the ladies.

"Julia," he complained, "do you know who that woman is?"

"Yes, Norval."

"But why? I mean, you can't . . . Damme, Julia, what are you two up to? They can't introduce you."

"We know that, Norval."

"Then why did you ask?"

"Because they do not know that we know."

"You're acting like a couple of ninnies."

"As Grandmama says, Norval, take no notice."

"She did say that."

"Then I expect you will take her advice."

He scratched his head. "It don't fadge with me." Nevertheless, he accompanied the curricle to Grosvenor Square, where they would await the arrival of Lord Effly and the Duke for supper.

When the two gentlemen did arrive and drinks were served, it was well after nine, and the Marchioness was not in her best spirits.

"Filmore has refused to allow dinner to be served," she snapped. "And no wonder. Nine is the hour he serves, not one minute before, not one minute after, but nine. I thought I had made that quite clear. Each morning he sets his kitchen clock according to the grandfather clock in the entrance hall. That clock, gentlemen, is never fast, never slow. When it says nine, it is nine. When it is nine, Filmore's dinner is served. When it is after nine, Filmore's dinner is ruined. Tonight, the soufflé has fallen, the almandaise sauce has curdled, the fowl is dry, the mutton is overdone, and the ices, melted. It is of little use to ask him to serve up what won't do. I fear we must, gentlemen, go hungry." She paced up and down the saloon, hitting the knuckles of one hand with her ebony fan.

"Grandmama, I am sure Filmore can be made to see reason." Julia was dressed in a pale blue dress with a low, square neck and short Spanish sleeves. In her hair she wore a blue plume that she had purchased that morning.

"Reason? Is it reasonable to serve a spoiled dinner? Is it reasonable to eat at the wrong hour?"

"Not good for the digestion," commented the Colonel, who sat before the fire staring at the carpet and longing for his dinner. "I think it was Hypocrites who

142

claimed that meals should always be taken at the same hours each day."

"Don't need no Greek to tell you that, Colonel. Stomach will do it every time." Norval had returned and stood by the fireplace in a suit so perfectly tailored and form-fitting, one might doubt that he could bend his knees to walk, not to mention sit. His jacket and eye patch were of violet and his necktie was in an impeccable knot. Because his starched collar was unusually high, he had difficulty seeing with his good eye those who were seated.

"We do humble apologize," said the Duke, truly sorry.

"Bring Filmore in here," commanded Lord Effly, "and I'll let him know what's what. You cannot let a chef run the household, Marchioness."

"Run my household? *I* run my household, and *I* hire a chef who serves when *I* please. And *I* choose that dinner be served at nine. Can't change the hour each night. An artist, that's what he is. Finest chef living. The Prince Regent comes to this house, to this very house, mind, for Filmore's cooking. You make light of artistry, sir. I wonder at your palate."

"I am sure Lord Effly meant no disrespect, Marchioness," apologized the Duke.

"I agree with Lord Effly," said Catherine, who looked exotic in a black velvet evening dress trimmed with silver cord. Silver feathers fluttered in her dark hair. The neck of her gown was more than common low so that the gentlemen's eyes often rested on that unexceptionable spot. "I think Filmore has tantrums far too often."

"Artistic expressions of true regret," snorted the Marchioness. "Any artist should express his temperament."

"Oh, Mother, do not say so," wailed Mrs. Hartman. "I am sure my nerves cannot stand many more such expressions."

"I quite agree with Grandmama," said Julia, who had caught sight of Filmore in the gallery.

"I, too," said Harriette on Julia's cue.

"Do you not think," Julia went on, "that we could prevail upon dear Filmore to just this once forgive us and serve us something to eat. We shall all understand it is not his best through our own fault. He will be like a soldier in battle, coming in to save the occasion."

"Exactly." The Marchioness nodded her approval. "If he understands how very sorry we are."

There was a tap on the door. "Enter."

"Filmore, Madame. I have reconsidered. Because of the great esteem I have for *some* members of this household," he gave a cutting look to Catherine and Mrs. Hartman, "I shall carry on. But just this once."

"That is certainly understood, Filmore," the Marchioness assured him.

"Well done, Filmore!" exclaimed Julia. "I knew we could count on you."

"*You* always can, Miss Julia." He left the room with an air of wounded pride.

"Damme," said Norval, "there's no end to the man's cheek."

"Hush," whispered Julia. "You know the chef is the most important member of the household." Without further comment, the party took partners to enter the dining hall.

Julia noticed during dinner that the Marchioness had sat Lord Effly to her right and now the old lady plied him with numerous questions. That Lord, accepting the attention as his due, was not loath to answer. He had the insouciant manner of one who appreciates his own worth and sat with an easy grace quite in contrast to Norval's rigid posture, exaggerated by the out-of-the ordinary stiff collar. Judging by appearance, Julia could not agree with Harriette's opinion of Lord Effly. He was decidedly attractive and throughout dinner made his charms available to Catherine as well as to the Marchioness. His aquiline nose, firm chin, sparkling eyes, and high forehead combined to give him a look of intelligence and dignity; yet his smile was disarming and boyish. Catherine seemed more attentive than usual to the conversation. But it was just that conversational style which put Julia off and caused her to agree with Harriette. For here was a pampered man. His replies to the Marchioness showed little depth, either of thought or character. He had a fine physique and was no doubt good at manly sports, so that the Duke could enjoy his company. However, tonight Julia watched Thomas as he listened attentively, said little, and noted both Catherine's and Harriette's reactions to his friend.

As the evening wore on, Julia found Lord Effly to be a worthy opponent at the card table, and his comments, though often self-centered, were sometimes witty. She also noticed Lord Effly's continued disregard of Harriette; not that he was rude, just disinterested. How could Thomas possibly want his sister to marry someone who ignored her? And what did he think of Lord Effly's attentions to Catherine? Although Thomas' scar now seemed barely noticeable to Julia, Catherine still appeared to be offended by it. Julia could not wait to hear her grandmother's views on the present company and was glad when the three gentlemen took their leave to go to Boodle's for a little serious gambling.

"Harriette's right," said the Marchioness later in her chamber. "Though I shouldn't think him 'odious.' Seems not much different from all the young blades. I suspect having him pushed on her made him look much worse than he ordinarily would have."

"I am sure you are right," agreed Julia. "I think the Nut Brown stains on his fingers and the bleary eyes after port were dramatic additions of her own imagination. She does have a lovely imagination."

"Yes, but we must see it doesn't get out of line."

"You do not mean she should marry him!"

"Certainly not. Stuffy sort of fellow who doesn't appreciate her. Can't have that. Did you meet any nice young men in the park today?"

"A few seemed agreeable. Lord Wigmore, Earl of Exeter, was introduced to us by Norval—Norval does, at times, make himself useful—and that man was very attractive and quite pleasant. I understand his friends call him 'Whip,' as he is said to handle the horses magnificently. I did think he paid decided attention to Harriette."

"Excellent. We must follow up on this Whip. Knew his grandfather. Fine fellow."

"But it will be rather awkward inviting him to supper with Lord Effly and Thomas about. And we cannot very well invite him and not them."

"We can if *you* are interested in him."

"And then Harriette can flirt with him? How very clever. I noticed Lord Effly paid scant attention to poor Harriette and did notice all of Catherine's better points."

"Even Norval's one eye couldn't miss those tonight. She's not loath to revealing her, uh, charms." They both laughed. "I should say, my girl, that a little scheming is now in order. For the good of all concerned, you understand."

"For the good of all concerned. And what fun we shall have."

"Now listen carefully, child." And the Marchioness told Julia her plan.

CHAPTER
TEN

The girls were not in London long before the seven
ladies at Almack's sent them vouchers of admission to
join their illustrious gathering at the Assembly Room
in King Street. The girls would be admitted to the
subscription ball on the very next Wednesday evening.
The three were in the morning room, opening invitations.

"I do not know why you fuss so," said Catherine.
"You will find it is no great privilege to be there, only
to *say* you have been, since it is all the thing. I doubt
anyone enjoys it as much as a private *soirée*, but we
should all be furious to be kept away. I find the cake
is often stale, and I do not fancy tea and bread and
butter at a dance."

"Is that all they serve?" asked Harriette, dismayed.

"Oh, there is usually lemonade. All quite dull. Of

course, it is livelier now that we do the waltz. How daring of Countess Lieven to have introduced it."

"I should like to have seen that," said Harriette. "Imagine, how bold! I think I shall quite faint away if I am ever asked to dance it."

"You do that," Catherine had to laugh, "and you will not be asked again. Imagine Lady Jersey attending to you as you lie prostrate on the dance floor."

"But imagine, being held in a man's arms. Lord Byron says the waltz is seductive."

"And voluptuous," put in Julia. "I quite look forward to doing it with Whip."

"*Mon dieu*, who is that?"

"The handsome Lord Wigmore, Earl of Exeter. He was introduced to us by Norval in the park. I declare I have a *tendre* for him."

"Do you indeed?" said Catherine. "*Fameux*. I understand he is quite a catch, and an Earl. I quite congratulate you, little sister, on your taste."

"Imagine being held in his arms," said Harriette, though it was not clear if she pictured Julia or herself supported by that gentleman. "I did detect he had a decided preference for you, Julia."

"Yes, I am certain of it. I made use of your half-lidded look, Catherine, and I think it quite won him. Though I should not tell you, or you may use it on him yourself."

"Have no fear, little sister. As you know, I am spoken for." She sighed. "Lord Effly is a great catch for you," Harriette.

Harriette made a face. "I find him stodgy."

"You must have the good breeding not to say so.

149

Your brother does intend you should marry him, so you must accept him in good grace. Your reaction is outside of enough. I find him gracious and an excellent conversationalist."

"I do not know that," said Harriette, "for he never speaks to me."

"You must make yourself more agreeable."

"Could you not help me, Catherine, to persuade Thomas to drop the matter?" pleaded Harriette.

"Yes, Catherine," enjoined Julia, "you could influence Thomas. It is unkind of him to want his sister to marry someone she does not love."

"We cannot all marry for love," Catherine answered bitterly.

"We all could if we chose," said Julia.

"My dear children, you understand nothing of life."

"I think you enjoy making it tragic for us all," Julia retorted.

"I shan't stay and listen to such accusations." She rose and left the room.

"You see, Harriette, there is nothing for it but to help ourselves."

"Your plan sounds excellent."

"Yes, I think it will do. I have already let Catherine know how I feel about the handsome Lord Exeter." She laughed. "Soon all the *beau monde* will know of my love and Lord Exeter will be so flattered, I fancy he will be around shortly. I do not think Catherine hurried away because of hurt feelings. She cannot wait to share her news. We shall soon hear the front doors close and catch a glimpse of Catherine on her way to make morning calls."

"This is such fun, Julia. It almost makes Lord Effly worth having on the scene. We have certainly added mystery, adventure, and love to our first season out. We cannot do much better than that."

"I think, my friend, we can do much better. Be patient. By the season's end, we shall have worked wonders."

The girls heard the front doors close, and a certain young lady entered her carriage to make her morning rounds.

Wednesday night arrived, and the long-awaited ball at Almack's commenced. Julia and Harriette wore new gowns of frothy white muslin. Catherine's gown, again kept a dark secret until the event, was of cherry velvet and white satin. The bodice was molded so tightly to her figure that no shoulder straps were necessary. Tiny puffed sleeves graced her arms but the whole of her bust and shoulders were exposed. Her black hair was in ringlets *à l'anglaise*. No one at Almack's commanded such attention.

"Catherine has done it again," Julia whispered from behind her fan to Harriette. "I notice Lord Exeter ogling what there is of her dress. And we thought our dresses so pretty and stylish. I am sure we were told they are in the peak of fashion."

"Yes, we were," sighed her friend. "I felt much prettier five minutes ago."

"I, too. Well, we must not think about that. It is vital to keep Lord Exeter from fawning over Catherine."

"But every man does."

"Well, *he* must not. He must be my beau so he can come to the house and you can flirt with him."

"What if he does not care for me? What if I do not care for him?"

"We must make the attempt. If you do not get to know other young men, you will not be able to judge what you do want."

To Julia's surprise, Whip did not long remain with Catherine but shortly made his way to her side and requested a dance. He had an open smile and boyish good looks. "Since meeting you in the park, I have looked forward to knowing you better. I understand that for a girl, you are clever with a whip."

Julia shrugged aside the demeaning phrase. "Perhaps you will one day care to see for yourself?" She would have great fun taking him for a drive. "But you must remember my dear friend Harriette whom you met with me?"

"Of course."

"She will be delighted to accompany us. I recall she mentioned how well you sit a horse."

"Did she?"

"Yes. She is without a doubt an uncommon fine judge of people and most popular with the men. For her to single you out for admiration is a decided compliment."

"I assure you, I am flattered by the attention." Lord Exeter danced gracefully, and Julia hoped that Harriette would be given permission by Lady Jersey to do the waltz so that her friend and Whip could do it together.

The country dance having ended, Julia took Whip

by the arm. "Come, let us join Harriette so that you can see for yourself what a charming friend I have."

"I should enjoy another dance with you."

"Oh no! I mean, you will want to enjoy a little conversation with Harriette first, I am convinced. Do not be shy with me. I noticed in the park that you were decidedly taken with her."

"I think you failed to note my eyes were on you."

"Indeed they were not. That is, they should not have been. I mean, oh dear, let us join Harriette." She led him to where her friend stood talking with Lord and Lady Chatterton and Lord Devon. "Harriette, dear, here is the gentleman you admired in the park. You remember Lord Wignore."

"Who could forget," said Harriette, just as she had practiced with Julia, although she did forget the half-lidded look. "I am so pleased to meet you again, Lord Wigmore, or may I call you Whip as your friends do?"

"By all means make it Whip."

"Of course, I shall dance with you, Lord Devon," said Julia to Norval.

"It's polite to wait to be asked," grumbled that lord.

"Why, you have been pestering me the entire evening. You know you have." She gave a little laugh.

"Haven't. Wouldn't. You're acting strange again, Julia."

"Come, come, Lord Devon, do not tease so." Julia took his arm and gave it a pinch.

"Ouch. You needn't pinch me."

Julia laughed and fanned herself. "Lord Devon is such a tease, is he not?"

"Decidedly so," said Harriette, also laughing. "Do

not pester Julia further. She will certainly dance with you."

"See here, don't you start in too. One of you telling faradiddles is quite enough."

"Come along, Norval. Such nonsense. What will Lord and Lady Chatterton think of you?"

"Of me? Why, I've been standing here having bread and butter sandwiches and tea. Seemed harmless enough until you came along."

Lady Chatterton laughed. "Norval, do not tease poor Julia any longer. Run along and dance."

"Poor Julia? Don't tease?"

Julia led him to the dance floor. "Norval, do be still," she murmured through clenched teeth.

"I'm to be still, am I?" he said in a loud voice.

"Yes," she whispered. "Can you not see what I am doing?"

"Yes. Making a fool of me."

"Hush. I am promoting a romance."

"You mean you're meddling again. You can't promote a romance. That's between the two people involved. How do you always get yourself in as some third party?"

"Norval, you offend me deeply."

"The feeling's mutual."

"You could at least understand what I am doing and help me along."

"I understand well enough, but I won't meddle. You're on your own there. And I was quite enjoying my sandwiches and tea. Rather good they were. Bread was fresh. Tea was strong."

"Do be still, Norval." Julia smiled at the other dancers.

"All very well for you to say. You weren't having none. Strong, hot tea. Very comforting. Helps the nerves, which is more than you do, Julia. Mother says I don't look well when you're up to some flummery."

"Your mother looks very happy at the moment because you are dancing with me. If you continue to scowl and grumble, you will upset her."

"That's a thought. Looks happy does she? How can you tell that?"

"If you would take off that primrose eye patch, you could see her sitting, talking to the Countess."

"Is she now? Good show. Great lady, my mother."

And so they danced but not for long. For soon other men were surrounding Julia, and she had trouble saving a dance for each. Her lively good humor, grace, and ease were a combination few men at Almack's wanted to forgo. But as she danced, she had an eye for Thomas. And as she danced, his scowl became more and more pronounced. Instead of joining in the festivities, he ignored even Catherine and watched Julia.

Finally, he came to where Julia stood, surrounded by dandies of the *haut ton*. "Miss Hartman, may I have a word with you?"

"Willingly, Duke. But first let me introduce you to these gentlemen." Because they were already known to the Duke, the introductions were dispensed with, and Thomas led Julia apart.

"I hate to be in a position to say this, but as your friend and future brother-in-law, I must speak." She said nothing as he paused but looked at him, her violet eyes wide. He cleared his throat. "Yes, well, that is to say, your conduct, and this is not pleasant for me to say, your conduct, Julia, is most unbecoming." She said nothing in reply as her innocent eyes watched him. "You do understand?"

"No."

"But you must understand."

"No."

"Confound it, Julia, you are not a child."

"No."

"Stop saying 'no.'"

"Yes."

"Damn your impudence."

"But Thomas, I listen quite willingly, and you fail to make yourself clear. Have I committed a solecism of which I am unaware?" Tears filled her violet eyes.

"Good lord, do not cry. Julia, this will not do. Come along over here where no one can see you. You cannot be seen crying at Almack's. I am sure no one has done so before."

"They have never been so sorely tried before. You tell me I have done something terrible, and you will not tell me what it is."

"Damnation. It is just that you have all those dandies hanging about you."

"What is wrong with that? Catherine does."

"She is an engaged woman, and I am here to protect her. Instead, I must spend my evening looking after you."

"But your sister has any number of men with her. Just look."

"Harriette will soon be Lady Effly, and her intended is here as well. You do not comprehend the situation is different for you?"

"No, I do not."

"You see. You persist in being obstinate."

"I am only dancing."

"But with whom? Young dandies you have only just met."

"When I went to introduce you, you knew them all. Is it not all right to dance with your friends?"

"No. I mean, these are acquaintances. That is different. I cannot vouch for their characters. And Catherine tells me you have a *tendre* for Lord Wigmore. You are too young to have a *tendre* for anyone. I forbid it. Will you give it up?"

"How can I tell my heart what to do, Thomas?"

"Then I must speak to the Marchioness tomorrow. It would appear she is the only one who has any control over you."

Julia smiled slightly, though two large tears worked their way down her pink cheeks. "Oh, she despairs of ever controlling me. Poor Thomas, there is really no one to whom you can speak. Perhaps you must dance with me yourself to keep me out of mischief."

"I fear that is the only way. Come along then. But do dry those tears first." He fumbled in his pocket for a handkerchief, and with what appeared to be a trembling hand, wiped them carefully from her cheeks. Then he led her to the dance floor, and those who watched her dance thought she was the most radiant young lady at the assembly. The Duke, too, they said, looked happier than he had in some time.

CHAPTER
ELEVEN

Julia was summoned by one of the footmen to the downstairs drawing room. She hurried along the dark passages and down the winding stairs to the large saloon, where she was surprised to find Witherspoon waiting.

"How good to see you, dear Witherspoon. Do you recall the many long hours we spent between life and death?"

"Could I ever forget, Miss Julia? You are a true friend. Terrible as those days were, I do miss them."

"I, too, Witherspoon, when I have a moment to reflect. Things happen so fast here. But it is exciting. I can quite see why Filmore, our chef, refuses ever to leave town."

"I must confess there is far more satisfaction dressing His Grace in London where all will see him than in the country where my work often goes unnoticed. Though not, I collect, by you."

Julia blushed.

"That brings me to my problem, Miss Julia. The Duke is not getting about as was his wont. He is, to put a word to it, sulking."

"Indeed, Witherspoon? And what is causing this sulking?"

"I can only suppose it is the old problem. His scar still troubles him, miss. I fear it is a sore trial to him."

"Poor Thomas. What can we do, Witherspoon?"

"I was hoping you or the Marchioness would have an answer, miss."

"The cream did make him look better."

"Yes, it did that. But the scar is still there, and he is ever conscious of it."

"I wonder . . ." Julia began to pace. "There is something I might try. No. And yet . . . Yes, it might work."

"Miss?"

"Witherspoon, I shall mesmerize him."

Witherspoon tried to suppress a laugh.

"Come, do not make light of it. I learned from the great Doctor Linse of Vienna. I was a student of his while he visited Lord Devon."

Witherspoon still seemed to have trouble keeping his lips in a straight line. "And have you practiced on anyone, miss?"

"Naturally. I was amazingly successful with Beau, and I should have been successful with Lord Devon as well if he had allowed himself to be mesmerized.

Even the greatest scientist cannot work against one's will, you understand."

"Yes, miss. But do you think His Grace will want to be mesmerized?"

"That will be the difficulty, Witherspoon. If he will once agree, I know I can succeed." She paced faster and faster as the idea took hold. Suddenly she stopped and shook Witherspoon's hand, much to his alarm. "You are a genius to have thought of this, my friend. Now that we have a plan, I shall certainly succeed. I can see that it was lack of a plan that held us back."

"I do hope that it will work, Miss Julia. After his attendance at Almack's last week, he has been decidedly dejected. He says he is left out of things. I cannot imagine what, since he is the one who often sets fashion. To have him grace her party is a hostess's fondest wish."

"You are right, Witherspoon. It is the scar. It is all in his mind, so we must work on the mind. Have no fear, he will soon be his old self."

"I am much relieved to hear you say that, miss. He always appears happier when you spend time with him."

"Does he? He no doubt likes the attention."

"I am certain he misses that. With Miss Harriette away and so very much in demand, if rumors are correct, he has only me now. He had become quite used to two young ladies attending to his every wish."

"Is he moping at home today?" Witherspoon nodded. "Then go, Witherspoon, and tell him I wish to see him at three this afternoon."

"And if he will not come?"

"Witherspoon, since it is our plan, we must make the decisions. It is your job to get him here."

He had to smile. "You give me more credit than is my due, Miss Julia. However, for you I am ready to attempt anything."

"Good. Three o'clock then. I count on you."

Witherspoon gave a low bow and went to carry out his mission.

At three o'clock, Julia was not surprised to be summoned to the Red Saloon on the second floor, where she wished the session to take place.

"Julia," the Duke exclaimed as she entered, "you are not ill?"

"Oh dear, do I look it?"

"Decidedly not. But I was told, that is, Witherspoon led me to believe . . ."

Julia smiled. "There must be some mistake. I was under the impression *you* were not well."

"Witherspoon is confusing things badly."

"I am glad you are here, Thomas. Will you be so kind as to do me a favor?"

"If it is in my power."

"Good. Will you, then, help me in my pursuit?"

"By all means. What is it?"

"Why, the study of mesmerism. Do you not remember? I studied under Doctor Linse from Vienna when he visited Lord Devon. I am considered quite good, but I do need practice from time to time."

"Practice?"

"In mesmerism."

"Do I understand that you wish to mesmerize me?"

"Yes. That is it. You will oblige, will you not? You are so very kind."

The Duke looked at her askance. "I never knew you to think me kind. Mesmerism. Tell me, what will you do?"

"I just talk to you, and you relax, and I give you suggestions. Afterwards you may not even be aware you have been mesmerized."

"What sort of suggestions?"

"What sort would you like?"

"I shouldn't particularly like any, but if I must oblige . . . No doubt you have already practiced upon all your family so that they can stand it no longer?"

Julia merely smiled.

"I think I should like you to tell me that I cannot notice my scar and that others cannot notice it either."

"That sounds good. Shall we commence?"

He laughed. "That's what you will say, is it? Well, go ahead. Your family seems as yet unharmed by your practice."

"You do not seem to have the utmost faith in me, Thomas. Nevertheless, we shall proceed."

Julia had him sit in a comfortable chair; then she commenced in her soft, mellifluous voice, especially reserved for mesmerism. Thomas's lips seemed to twitch a little at first, but he soon settled down and became very relaxed. Finally, when he seemed in a deep mesmeric sleep, Julia commenced her suggestions.

"You will begin to realize that you are making everyone unhappy by your constant concern over your scar. You will understand that the scar is noticed by no one but yourself. You will pay no attention to it. Furthermore, you will not let your family and friends, who love you, see that you notice it. You will be cheerful and optimistic. You will no longer sulk but will go dancing and riding in the park and enjoy life." She paused to think if she had covered everything.

"Now you will gradually awaken. I shall count from five to one. When I reach one, you will open your eyes and feel happy and content. You will no longer think about your scar or even notice it. Five, four, take a deep breath, three, two, one."

Thomas blinked his eyes. "When are you going to practice on me, Julia? Though I must say, I am so happy I hope you do not spoil my good mood. I feel so very content about life."

"Really! This is capital. Thomas, I think I shall not practice today after all."

"But I am quite willing."

"It is very kind of you. But we shall do it some other time. Let us send for tea."

"By all means. Then we must have a ride in the park."

"Oh, do you think so?"

"I never before saw you so pleased about a ride in the park. We must have them more often."

"Thomas," her violet eyes were wide, "life is quite remarkable."

He laughed. "Indeed it is."

CHAPTER
TWELVE

"Really, Stanfield, your pacing is annoying." The Marchioness beat a tattoo with her fan on the knuckles of one hand. The Duke found that annoying as well but declined to say so.

"I cannot understand, Marchioness, why you could possibly think Lord Effly would be a suitable match for Julia. Where could you have come by such a thought?" He commenced pacing again, and the Marchioness continued her tattoo.

"You must admit that Lord Effly pays scant attention to your sister, and she cannot abide him. It's clear that Julia is the one he's concerned about. We can surely make an equally suitable match for Harriette. I, sir, cannot see your objection to Lord Effly and Julia. I seem to recall that he is a good friend of yours, and now suddenly you object to him."

"I certainly do not object to him. He is a perfect match for Harriette. Wonderful fellow. Excellent sportsman. Couldn't ask for a finer brother-in-law. But as for Julia, that is out of the question. They are not right for each other. In any event, that Whip character . . ."

"Your good friend as well.".

"No longer. He hangs about after Julia in a disgraceful manner. I cannot think you would allow it."

She chuckled. "What can one do where sentiment is involved?"

"Sentiment? You speak of sentiment? Nonsense."

"You may be right. Young people are often fickle."

"And if she is so taken with Wigmore, how do you propose to make a match with Effly? She believes in romance and all that that means in storybooks. You will never force her to the altar with someone she does not love."

"Yes, she is rather like your sister in that."

"My sister! Certainly not. But back to our subject, Marchioness. I think you are letting this whole thing with Julia get out of hand."

"What would you have me do?"

"I suppose she could be sent back to the country."

"At the height of the season and her first at that? Nonsense. I meant, whom would you have her marry?"

"Marry! I cannot think of Julia married. She is much too young and frivolous. She needs several seasons out before any serious decision is made in that direction."

"Is she not a few months older than Harriette?"

"Marchioness, this is outside of enough." The Duke stopped before the august lady. "Harriette has been schooled for marriage. She is not filled with the wild notions that occupy Julia's mind. There can be no possible comparison made."

The Marchioness' eyes twinkled. "Perhaps you're right, Stanfield. Nevertheless, I shan't be surprised to see Julia affianced before the close of the season. It is not in a lady's best interest to let too many seasons go by without making a choice, and there seem to be more eligible young men about this year than I recall seeing during any other."

"I see you mean to take advantage of the situation."

"Can't afford not to, young man. I still think if you weren't so stubborn and I could get her to fancy Effly, it would be a good thing."

"Never."

"Well, you think about it."

"I tell you, I don't have to think about it."

"You'll change your mind. People always come around to thinking I'm right."

"I shall hate to disappoint you, Marchioness, but this is one time you will fail." The Duke gave a stiff bow and turned, infuriated by the Marchioness' deep chuckle that followed him into the hall and down the stairs.

"Oh, dear." Harriette quickly shut the drawing room door after peeping out. "It is my brother coming down the stairs and with a face as long as you can imagine. I swear he was abominable at the Devonshires' ball last night. He is such a watchdog over us both that he is sending away any men who are suitable. He did everything possible to keep Whip from us both. In fact, I think he guards you even more closely than me."

Beau yawned, jumped off Julia's lap, stretched, and sniffed at Harriette. "Dear Beau, you are not such a watchdog, are you?"

Julia laughed. "He could not stay awake long enough. You must admit, your brother has been decidedly more agreeable since I mesmerized him. At least, until lately. Perhaps it is wearing off. I suppose it must wear off at some time or other."

Just then the doors swung open, and the Duke entered unannounced. "I see you two are hatching plots to deceive me. I no sooner turn my back on one of you than the other is in trouble."

"Trouble!" sputtered Julia. "Duke, we are the soul of propriety on every occasion."

"Hah!"

"That is what Grandmama would say."

"She should say something more and stop your idle flirting with every man in London."

"But Thomas, dear," interposed Harriette, "we flirt with only . . ."

"Do not tell me. Do you think I cannot see for myself? It is that Whip character."

"Your friend," Julia smiled.

"And it's damned strange you are both flirting with him. That is highly improper in itself."

"Nonsense, Thomas," said Harriette. "He is your friend. Would you have us ignore your friend?"

"You might remember that when it comes to Effly, or for that matter poor Norval. You ignore whom you choose."

"Lord Effly ignores me, Thomas."

"That he does, Duke," added Julia.

"Stop calling me Duke."

"I am just being respectful."

"You are *not* being respectful."

"Come, Thomas," Julia patted the settee on which she sat. "Sit down and let us talk." The Duke reluctantly did as he was bid. "We were getting on so famously for a time," she went on. "Rides in the park, shopping sprees. What has happened?"

"Happened? It's your outrageous flirting; that's what has happened. I cannot keep up with you both."

Julia motioned to Harriette to slip away. As Harriette did so, Julia lowered her voice slightly. "Thomas, you look a little tired. Why not put your head back and relax?"

The Duke glanced at her, an odd expression on his face. To Julia's surprise, he did as he was bid.

"That is good. You are very, very tired. You want to relax. You feel your muscles relaxing." His facial muscles did not seem to respond to this command, but Julia took no notice. "Your eyes are open, but they are growing heavy. They want to close." The Duke's eyelids drooped. "When your eyes close, you will go into a deep mesmeric trance." His eyes gradually shut.

"Now you picture yourself in a lovely setting, perhaps by the sea. You have no cares. You are so calm, so happy. You go deeper and deeper into your mesmeric trance. Down and down. So calm. So happy.

Now you picture yourself in London, happy, carefree. You are enjoying all the activities. You are nice to everyone and have no more fits of the sullens."

The Duke looked amazingly peaceful and happy. Julia paused for a moment; then her face lit up with a mischievous smile.

"You are back in the drawing room with me. You take my hand." The Duke took her small hand in his own, his eyes still shut.

"You put my hand to your lips." He lifted it to his lips and kissed it, lingeringly. Then, without command, he turned it palm up and kissed it several times so that she gasped.

This was so extraordinarily successful that, although giddy, she decided on further commands. "You now, Thomas, have an overpowering urge to take me into your arms. You move closer to me."

Without a moment's hesitation, the Duke obeyed. Julia paused again, stunned at her own success. The Duke sat motionless.

"You," she whispered shyly, "you hold me as if I were the only person in the world, the one you truly love."

She had barely uttered her command when a strong arm supported her and a large hand rounded upon her full young breast. She could say no more. His nearness, his strength, his very scent made her head reel. Yet it would seem the last command was amazingly powerful, for the Duke's lips were on her own, forcing hers gently open. While fire surged through her body, his hands obeyed her order.

There was a knock on the door. "You must stop,

Thomas. You must stop." She had barely time to pull herself away before Benton entered.

"Beg pardon, miss. His Grace's man is here with an important message for the Duke." A frown came over Thomas's face.

"Do go, Benton. The Duke will be free in one minute." When the doors were shut, she turned to him. She must carefully bring him out of his trance. "Thomas, you will gradually awaken as I count backwards. You will recall nothing of what has occurred but will remember to be cheerful. And, oh, Thomas, you will be a little kinder to me. Now take a deep breath. Five, four, take another breath, three, two, one. Open your eyes.

"Well, Thomas, how do you feel?" She smiled on him radiantly.

"Cheated."

"Cheated? Then the message must have to do with business. Witherspoon is outside with a message for you."

"And how can you know that, or are you now studying reading of the mind?"

"I shan't tell, but you must go along. You do feel happier, do you not?"

The Duke had to laugh. "Much, much happier. I think, Julia, you are very good for me. I talk to you for a short while—and to tell the truth, I cannot even recall our conversation—yet I go away feeling refreshed and happy. How do you explain it?"

"I cannot, Thomas. But I am so very pleased." Her glowing face and sparkling eyes made her remark redundant.

A second knock on the door brought the Duke to the hallway and off to check with his estate manager. When he was safely gone, Harriette reappeared. "How did he respond?"

"Splendidly. I think we shall have a little peace for awhile. Only . . ." She trailed off.

"What?"

"Never mind. We were interrupted, that is all. It would have been so nice had we not been interrupted."

"Julia, may I confide in you?"

"Of course. Are we not best friends?"

"Yes, but this is so delicate. You see, I think I have developed a *tendre*."

"How delightful. Who is he?"

"Whip."

"But that is what we had planned."

"Yes. I know it is ever so unromantic to go according to plans. However, at first I thought it was you he cared for. Yet after last night . . ." She blushed.

"And you have waited so long to tell me? What happened?"

"He declared an undying passion for me."

"No!"

"Yes! He said I am everything he has always dreamed of."

"I do not doubt you are."

"He said I am beautiful. No one has ever said that to me before."

"But you are, Harriette. He merely shows good taste."

"There is more." Harriette looked crestfallen and

sank upon a Jacobean tapestried chair. Julia, sitting on the floor at her feet, prepared to hear the entire tale.

"I was forced, quite naturally, to tell him about Lord Effly."

"What else could you do?"

"He says the answer is to elope."

"Elope? With a license from Gretna Green? Whatever would your brother say? Not even my grandmama would approve of that." Julia knelt before her friend. "I cannot permit you to do anything so foolish. I understand that your situation is desperate. Nevertheless, we must bring the desired results about in the acceptable manner. You cannot, Harriette, cause scandal."

"Please do not scold me, Julia. I am beside myself."

"I quite understand. This is worthy of a novel by Mrs. Radcliffe. I can see now why you are so forlorn, and I am happy that you are sharing your misery with me. We must think of a plan."

"I knew you would have an answer, Julia."

"I do not have one yet, but we shall think of something. We must see the Marchioness."

"What will she think of me?"

"That you are very wise to do nothing foolish and to confide in me." She arose and gave Harriette a hug. "I must say, I am delighted that Whip has declared himself." She was rather surprised as well, but kept that to herself. "Come along. Grandmama will know what to do."

* * *

"Bit sudden, ain't it?" asked that lady after being told the news.

"But Marchioness, great passions overwhelm one suddenly, do they not?" ventured Harriette meekly.

"I know nothing of great passions, girl, sudden or otherwise. Seems to me in my day we just fell in love in quite the usual way. These great passions are so tiresome. I suppose you, Harriette, have a great passion for this Whip character?"

"Decidedly."

"I knew it. Queer in the attic, the lot of you. I should have left you at your brother's. I hope you ain't going to tell *him* anything about a great passion."

"Grandmama, it is ever so romantic."

"Romance, fiddlesticks. When that blazing fire goes out, you'll find those ashes mighty cold. Better to make do with a nice little fire that stays cozy."

"Grandmama!"

"I know. I know. I'm not romantic. So you like this Whip character and he likes you back. That's a fair start. Could do worse. I've been checking on him."

"Marchioness!" Harriette's hands flew to her cheeks.

"Don't be so missish. A Brutus cut to the hair and an elegant tie to the neckcloth and you girls are swept away without a thought to living with the man. Let's just see what we know about him. He's a nice enough looking chap, by the way."

"I think him positively handsome," murmured Harriette.

"Yes, well, you would. Great passions do wonders to features."

Julia laughed. "Grandmama, that is not fair. You

know you think him handsome." The Marchioness had to chuckle.

"To go on, his family is beyond reproach, and he's done well at Oxford, which is more than can be said for most young men these days. He gambles lightly, is not in debt, and is spoken well of by his peers and by his servants. It's the latter that count. They get you up in the morning and put you to bed at night and know what sort of person you really are."

"Grandmama, how did you find all that out?"

"Never you mind, young lady. Of course, if you are clever, you might ask yourself if there is anyone who is anyone whom I do not know; and being clever you will answer yourself that there is not. That fact makes obtaining information relatively easy. At any rate, I find nothing that Stanfield can object to in Wigmore."

"Except that he prefers Lord Effly," said Harriette, dejected. "He feels he has given Lord Effly his word."

"It's not *his* word but *your* word that matters. Run along girls. I shall give this some thought. And don't do anything foolish."

"No indeed, Marchioness. Thank you." Harriette, knowing her brother's stubborn nature, could not feel joyous at this promise of help.

The girls went back to the drawing room and found the rest of the family, with Norval, seated around the fire. "Really, girls, I have only just heard." Mrs. Hartman accosted them as they entered. Harriette looked alarmed.

"Come, Mama, what have you heard?" asked Julia, good-naturedly.

"Something about a *tendre*," said the Colonel as he

sniffed at a cigar, cut its end, and took deep drags in lighting it.

"How could you?" squeaked Harriette.

"Julia told me quite openly," said Catherine, lazily.

"I never did," said Julia as her friend eyed her accusingly.

"Didn't tell *me*." Norval appeared angry. "Should think I'd have been told." He struck an injured pose beside the fireplace. Julia had to admit to herself that he looked quite elegant in the tightest possible pantaloons and mauve jacket and eye patch. "What about my expectations? What about my mother?"

"Oh, *that tendre!*" exclaimed Julia.

"Don't tell us there's more than one," snapped Norval. "One's outside of enough. Can't go around having *tendres* like they was mild flirtations."

"I do feel, Julia, you might have let your mother know. And with someone called Whip! What will people say? He sounds like a tiger. Do say he's not a tiger. I could not bear it if he is a tiger." Mrs. Hartman blew her nose on a lace handkerchief.

"Of course he is not a tiger, Mama."

"That at least is some consolation. But what is to be done?"

"Why, not a thing," said Julia brightly.

"Julia, pet, I think we should meet this Whip," said the Colonel congenially. He had never fancied Norval as a member of the family. Perhaps if Julia married, Norval would take himself off to some other household.

"What a good idea, Papa. We must have Whip here. Then you will see what a fine young man he is."

"I cannot believe it," insisted Mrs. Hartman. "Anyone with a name like that has little good in him."

"But Mama, I have explained the name," said Catherine crossly as Julia and Harriette stared her down.

"It doesn't signify. I do not like him."

"*Grands dieux!* You have not yet met him," Catherine persisted.

"I shall dislike him when I do meet him. I do not know that I care to meet him. My younger daughter. First season. Barely out. What is he thinking of?"

"You brought the girl here to marry her off," said the Colonel. "Why else are we here? I could be in the country now enjoying life instead of being cramped up in this gloomy monstrosity. And for what? To get your daughters married."

"*My* daughters? It is sorry you would be, Colonel, if you had them on your hands as spinsters."

The Colonel winked at Julia. "Then let's get this one off our hands at once. I insist we invite that Whip character."

Julia had to laugh. "Capital, Papa."

"See here, Colonel," interjected Norval. "I do believe you're forgetting my suit."

"But hasn't Julia turned you down, Norval? Several times?"

"That don't fadge with me. She's got some growing up to do. That's what Mother says. She'll take to me eventually. Just see if she don't."

"Do not be idiotish, Norval. You must be my friend, or I should have no friend to turn to in time of need."

"I do see that, Julia. But I don't see why Harriette can't be your friend."

"Oh, she is, but you are a longtime friend who is older and wiser than Harriette. Marrying you would cost me your friendship."

"I don't quite follow you. And I don't think Mother would see it that way."

"She must be brought round."

"Odd, Julia. She says *you* must be brought round."

"What do you think of Whip, Norval?" asked Catherine gaily.

"Can't like him so much now as I did. Nice enough fellow, though. Bad shot, but is smashing with the ribbons."

"You girls all look very jolly for having upset your mother so," interjected Mrs. Hartman. "I cannot take it as kind on your part to say you like Whip, Norval. You should be demanding a duel, not making pleasantries about him."

"Calm yourself, Clarissa," said the Colonel, a bit perturbed because Norval was so fond of dueling.

"A duel? Me duel with Whip? He just ain't that good. Think how boring it would be. Everyone would know I could hit him and would know he couldn't hit me. Where's the fun in that, damme? It's not sportsmanlike."

Mrs. Hartman sniffed. "A duel is not supposed to be *fun*, Norval. It is deadly serious. You are supposed to be very angry."

"Yes." Norval scratched his head. "Mother says I'm very angry. Odd. Must be showing more anger than I feel. Little miffed at Julia is all. Sooner duel with her than Whip. She's a better shot."

"Thank you, Norval."

"Not at all, Julia."

"Don't talk of duels," said the Colonel. "Was it Novara or Pythagoras who spoke of the harmonious interaction in nature? Might have been Copernicus. No matter. Man was not meant to duel but to live in harmony. You should take up the philosophers, Norval. Give you no end of comfort."

"Sounds deuced boring, sir. I tried to get them down once but got all the names wrong."

"Names don't mean a thing, my boy. Meaning's what counts."

"The meanings escaped me, don't you know. I flatter myself I'm not bookish."

"Colonel, something must be done," wailed Mrs. Hartman. "I feel very put upon."

"Mustn't feel that way, my love. No one would put upon you, I'm sure."

"'I have been obliged to take a little hartshorn and water each day this past week. Young people act so reckless today. It is an impossible task to be a mother."

"Now, Mama," said Julia, "do not fly into a miff. We are all quite up to the mark. I cannot think why you complain."

"I cannot think why either, since it does me no good. One daughter will not announce her engagement; the other takes up with a tiger Whatever will happen next?"

"Come, love, let us walk in the garden."

"Colonel, I am sorely tried."

"Yes, my dear. Come along. Only think what Socrates would say."

"I cannot at the moment, Colonel, care what he would say. I am sure he never had to concern himself with daughters during the London season. It is all very well for your philosophers. They have not had to bear my trials."

The young people could not help laughing once the Colonel had left with Mrs. Hartman on his arm.

"Mama will persist in calling Whip a tiger." Julia chuckled.

"What is she to think," complained Norval, "when you announce a grand *tendre* for him and never bring him around?"

"I did no such thing."

"My dear little sister, I heard you myself."

"You are not supposed to gossip, Catherine."

"Oh, yes, she was supposed to. Do you not remember?" asked Harriette innocently.

"I was supposed to what?"

"Never mind," Julia interposed. "Harriette is thinking of a novel we have read, but the plot is much too complicated to bring up now. I think the only answer is to invite Whip here for Mama to meet. Once she sees him, she will understand he is a lord. His manners are unexceptionable."

"Yes, he is so gallant," sighed Harriette.

"I don't much like the idea. Can't think mother will either. Rum business this, Julia. Never met anyone with so many ramshackle notions."

"It is better than having no notions at all, Norval," Julia answered pointedly.

"Come, do not quarrel," said Catherine. "We shall invite Whip tonight with Thomas. I am sure Mother

179

will take to him. And we must be certain to include Lord Effly for Harriette."

"Not on my account, pray," Harriette responded rapidly.

"But we must, my dear. We cannot offend him. I myself find him filled with *joie de vivre*."

Julia and Harriette looked at each other in surprise.

"Well, I ain't going to duel with Whip no matter what," insisted Norval. "Hurt my reputation. Have to be sportsmanlike. Crazy notion. A duel wouldn't have come up if it wasn't for your *tendre*, Julia. You're even more trouble in town than you are in the country." Norval was getting red in the face in an effort to look down at Julia from above his starched collar.

"Do be still, Norval. You are acting like a peagoose." Julia answered him. "I wish you would stop lecturing me. No one expects you to fight a duel."

"Your mother does. Just heard her. You were here yourself. Don't tell me you didn't hear her, 'cause it won't fadge. Your flummery is outside of enough."

"I agree with Julia, Norval." Catherine yawned. "Do be still. *J'ai mal à la tête*."

"A headache is it? Whip would have a fine one were I to duel with him."

"Pour l'amour de dieu!" Let us hear no more of this." Quite forgetting her Grecian pose, Catherine flopped onto a chair. "Julia, do send off a missive immediately. I should like to get to know Lord Wigmore better."

"I shall be happy to write to him for you, Julia," said Harriette, rising. "And you may write to Lord Effly."

Catherine interrupted her. "As the elder and an engaged woman, it is better that I write to Lord Effly. However, you, Julia, should write your own love notes."

"Love notes, is it? Never wrote *me* a love note. I say, Julia, do you write love notes to Whip? Maybe I *should* provoke a duel."

"Of course not, Norval."

"I think you should," said Catherine, "if it is so very serious. *Inutile de vous dire*, I write the occasional note to Lord Stanfield."

Julia reddened. "I was not aware of that. Are they . . . are they amorous?"

"Do not act caper-witted. I shall certainly not discuss my intimate notes with you."

"Intimate notes, indeed! Come along, Harriette. We shall write our own intimate notes."

"Damme, Julia, you oughtn't to be writing intimate notes to anyone."

But Julia flounced out of the room without a backward glance.

CHAPTER
THIRTEEN

In due course the notes had been written, the guests had arrived and supped, and now they sat chatting in the long drawing room. The Marchioness, more at ease at a card table, fidgeted.

"And you are certain," said Mrs. Hartman, though she had been assured numerous times during dinner, "that you are not a tiger, Lord Wigmore? You are, indeed, a lord?"

With difficulty, Harriette suppressed a giggle.

"I assure you, Mrs. Hartman, that I am Lord Wigmore, Earl of Exeter." He had a pleasant manner, usually seeing the humor in a situation. Now his eyes twinkled.

"Yet you let your friends call you Whip like you were common riffraff. I wish you will drop that name."

"Come, ma'am. I cannot easily do that. For one thing, people are too used to the epithet, and for another, I quite enjoy it. I am very proud of my driving skill and gratified that my friends notice and approve."

"The young scamps today have different ways, my love."

"Yes, Colonel. It was so different in our day. Why then your entire family would be in disgrace."

"Nonsense, Clarissa," snapped the Marchioness. "I once had a lover, called himself 'Facer.' Facer Fawley. Loved to box."

"Grandmama, truly?" Julia's eyes lit up as did Harriette's.

"I was young and beautiful once, my girl. Where do you think you get your good looks from?"

Julia laughed. "But what about Grandpapa?"

"Oh, that was before his time."

"Mother, do be still. How shocking. How can you tell the girls such stories, and visitors as well? You will offend their finer feelings. I am certain it is all pure gammon."

"Not a word of it. Fact of the matter is, I had several lovers before your grandpapa. And the cicisbeos after I married!"

"Mother, pray do stop." Mrs. Hartman laughed nervously. "This is surely a farradiddle."

"Hah!" was all the great lady retorted, and the young people laughed.

"Come, my dear, man is a social being. I am certain that the Dutchman Grotius agreed with Aristotle on

183

that point. We all have our friendships, don't you know."

"Fiddle, Colonel. I have had enough of your philosophers for one evening. We had a steady stream of them throughout supper."

"It's common sense, my love."

"I do not want common sense. I want social mores as they once were."

"Daughter, you are unaware of what they once were." The Marchioness emitted a deep, gravel-voiced chuckle.

"I do believe, my dear, that I quite swept you off your feet before you had a chance to have other amours."

Mrs. Hartman fanned herself and gave a nervous laugh.

During this conversation, Catherine and Lord Effly talked quietly, ignoring the others, and Harriette looked on, wide-eyed, subdued by her brother's presence. The Duke sat silently, once in a while raising his quizzing glass to his eye.

"Stanfield," said Norval, adjusting the maroon patch over his bad eye, "you've been more than common quiet lately. Anything the matter?"

The Duke frowned at having the company's attention drawn to him.

"I think a certain young lady could be responsible." Mrs. Hartman directed her gaze at Catherine.

"I beg to differ," responded Norval. "It's only business matters that put a man in the gloom."

Lord Wigmore laughed. "Cheer up, old fellow. Your friends will not let you down. And only think, if you lose one estate, you can fall back on the other four. Though I must admit, you will feel mighty cramped."

At this the Duke had to smile. "You know I do not care a fig for money matters, at least not enough to bore my friends with."

"It's the weight of being head of the family," Norval decided. "I feel it keenly myself. Mother says it can bring on the migraine."

"Nonsense, Norval." Julia's eyes twinkled. "You have never had the migraine in your entire life."

"But I could, don't you know. Though I'm inclined to think if I did get an attack, it would be your doing."

"Norval, how ungracious." Julia noticed the Duke chuckling.

"Come, children," snapped the Marchioness, "you are boring me to death. I should have thought you young people could handle a more lively conversation. I collect you, Whip, was to ride out with Julia?"

"Damme, that's a piece of conversation could well have been avoided!" exclaimed Norval. "I don't like the idea by half. I won't have my intended driving about town with a stranger. Bound to be talk."

"Intended?" The Duke rose and towered over Norval. "Pray what do you mean by that, sir?"

"Well, it's understood. I mean . . ." He halted under the Duke's powerful gaze.

"See here, what a lark. A stranger, am I?" said Lord Wigmore, merrily. "You must show me how you handle the ribbons, Julia. Will tomorrow suit you?"

"Admirably, Whip. And I look forward to observing your apparently unequaled style."

"Norval is right," said the Duke, abruptly. "This will not do at all."

"The very thing I said," grumbled Norval. "I say it, and you jump on me. Then you say the very same thing. You're acting touched in the upper works, Stanfield. Mother has observed it. Don't think she hasn't."

Julia laughed. "Your mother is a very observant lady, Norval."

"And you've been acting cocklebrained yourself."

"Fiddle, Norval."

The Marchioness chuckled. "I now think the conversation is becoming lively."

"Mother, do not encourage the child."

"Come, Clarissa, my love. Let us go to bed and leave the young people to sort this out."

"Really, Colonel, I think you should take a stand."

"But, my dear, you might not like my stand. Come along." He led his wife out. "Herder, my dear, was a great believer in following one's feelings." The doors closed, and the Marchioness was left as chaperone.

As sometimes happens in the game of love, especially when a number play at the game, partners chance to change. So it was on the following afternoon. Before the others were aware of what was happening, Harriette was in the curricle beside Whip. Julia took the reins of Lord Effly's horses and suggested a race. Catherine, Norval, and the Duke were left to look on, dismayed and not altogether pleased.

Whip responded to the challenge with delight, though Lord Effly did not care to have his rather ner-

186

vous chestnuts driven by a lady. Nonetheless, he sat beside Julia, a look of resignation on his face. If his intended was to ride with Whip, he had better be a party to the occurrence.

"Come, Norval. You must act as starter," called Julia.

"I'll do no such thing."

The Duke had to grin. "I shall start you off, you rogue. And see that you win." He raised his hat in the air. Both drivers were poised. He lowered the hat, and the two took off at a respectable clip, the horses aware of experts at the ribbons. There were no cheers, however, for this race. The Duke chuckled as he watched the curricles disappear in clouds of dust. "Child's play," complained Catherine. "Think what Mother will say," grumbled Norval.

"Oh, for heaven's sake, Norval, do not be such a goose as to tell her."

"Catherine, you are out of sorts." The Duke's lips twitched and his eye twinkled.

"You encourage my sister in all her nonsense."

"By God, Stanfield, I think you do."

"I just said that, Norval," snapped Catherine.

"It is a harmless bit of fun. You must admit that the two girls certainly cannot get into any trouble with Whip and Effly. On their own, there is no telling what will come next."

"You have a point there," admitted Norval, scratching his head while attempting to digest what had been said.

"Thank you, Norval. From you that is high praise."

"Is it now?" Norval looked very pleased.

"I still think it is foolishness. What are we supposed to do while they ride about the park?" Catherine pulled absently on a lace handkerchief she held.

"We could enjoy each other's company?" suggested the Duke, sardonically.

"We do that, *ne pensez-vous pas?*"

The Duke looked thoughtful. He had not anticipated a direct question. Avoiding any definite reference to their relationship had been the accepted course. Now Catherine seemed to be challenging him on new ground. "I wonder," he said briefly.

"You certainly look sullen, Catherine, if we're to be enjoying each other's company. You ain't looking so happy yourself, Stanfield. Rum sort of race, this. No one even determined on a course. And here we stand. Is this to be the finish line?"

"I have no idea," said the Duke.

"Precisely what I mean. There are supposed to be rules laid down. With Julia and Harriette involved, there's certain to be some flummery."

The Duke could not help laughing. Catherine looked at him askance. "I cannot see what is so humorous."

"They are rather funny." He was still laughing.

"I have never found my sister, nor yours, I might add, funny. What they do is pure skimble-skamble and idiotish. They are mere children filled with romantic notions."

"I suppose you are right." Stanfield sighed.

"I can't see why they haven't circled round here," complained Norval, who was apparently not enjoying the present company as much as he might. "Leave us all to ourselves. Oughtn't to run off that way. Hair-brained thing for them to do. Shouldn't have allowed it, Stanfield."

"See here, how could I have stopped them?"

"Ought to have some control over your sister. At least Julia isn't with Whip."

"I noticed that," said the Duke slowly. "Now that I think, she got directly in beside Effly without so much as a glance at Wigmore."

"I collect you are right." Catherine looked agitated. "One minute she is writing love notes to Whip and declaring a grand *tendre* for him; the next, she is flirting with Lord Effly. This cannot be supported."

"Love notes!" Stanfield looked furious.

"I said she shouldn't," put in Norval. "You encouraged her, Catherine. Put the idea into her head. I heard you."

"Love notes!"

"Stanfield," said Norval, "don't stand there repeating yourself. *I'm* the one who should complain. Hope she didn't write none to Effly."

"Do not say so, Norval." Catherine looked pale.

"Already have said so. No doubt about it, she **has** taken to writing love notes."

"Something must be done," insisted Catherine.

The Duke turned to his affianced. "You seem unusually agitated over what is Julia's and Harriette's concern." He eyed her questioningly until she blushed. "It would seem the young ladies have decided to switch lovers. And we are left, as I suggested earlier, to enjoy each other's company."

"What about me? I ain't enjoying nothing. Julia is my friend. I've known her longer than anyone except for you, Catherine."

"Do be still, Norval. Oh, what are we to do?"

"Why, nothing," answered the Duke, "but wait to see the outcome of the race."

CHAPTER
FOURTEEN

In due course, Lord Wigmore's curricle returned to the starting place, but not before the three who waited had determined to do so no longer and were walking to the Duke's carriage.

"Hallo, where are you off to?" shouted Whip, driving after them. The horses drew up, the curricle's two occupants looking radiant.

The Duke nodded. "We had given you up. Pray what has happened to the others? Or have you, living up to your reputation, left them far behind? This must be the longest race in history."

"You mean they haven't appeared?" Harriette glanced at Whip. "But we left them, oh goodness, ever so long ago."

"Did you, indeed?" Stanfield's lips curled in a sneer. "And what, pray, was your course?"

"I cannot rightly say we had a course." Whip looked

guilty. "It was all in good fun, Stanfield. I mean, off we went."

"But where are they?" Catherine demanded.

Whip and Harriette looked at each other again and burst out laughing. "We simply do not know," he managed to get out between spasms of laughter.

"See here," said Norval. "This ain't done. Looks bad and all that."

The Duke glowered. Finally, both Harriette and Whip noticed his face and became silent. "Are we to expect them back here?" asked Stanfield in measured tones.

"I, I do not know," Harriette answered falteringly.

"You say you left them. Exactly what does that mean? Were you that far ahead, or did they take a different course?"

Whip rubbed his hands together uneasily. "Look here, Stanfield, you are making a great thing of a harmless race."

"Harmless? Where are the other two? And you have not answered my question."

"They turned off," said Harriette meekly.

"*They* turned off," sputtered Norval. "You mean *Julia* turned off. Just like something she'd do."

"Do hush, Norval," said Catherine, her voice quavering. "Oh, where can they have gone?"

"In the direction of Bloomsbury." said Whip, looking down at the reins.

"Bloomsbury!" The others shrank from the Duke's roar. "Nobody goes to Bloomsbury. It is a totally unacceptable place."

"My God," said Norval. "Julia's been trying to get me to take her there."

"And Effly has done so." Stanfield was livid.

"Surely he would not," insisted Catherine.

"Oh, would he not? Where are they then?"

"I knew she'd be up to something," said Norval.

"I shall have to call Effly out," said the Duke.

"Oh, no!" Catherine felt faint and had to be helped into Harriette's seat in the curricle. "I refuse to let you call him out," she stammered.

"So do I," announced Norval. "It's my place to do it."

"Oh, Norval, you cannot. I shall not allow it," Catherine protested.

"See here," said Whip, "they are just taking a little drive."

"Thanks to you," said the Duke.

"Perhaps if we go back to Grosvenor Square we shall find they have returned."

"Excellent solution, Harriette." She blushed prettily with Whip's praise.

"It's no good waiting here," said Norval.

The Duke led the others to his barouche while Harriette gave a backward glance at Catherine in Whip's curricle. Soon the two carriages had made their way to the Marchioness' house, but when the young people entered the long drawing room, they did not discover the two truants.

"Not here," said Stanfield, pacing up and down before the large fireplace.

"If you would all be seated, I shall summon the Marchioness," said Benton.

"No need," the Duke replied. But apparently Benton thought there was every need, and he hurried away. Soon he was back, announcing the Marchioness.

"So I have unexpected guests," said that lady drily when she entered. "To what do I owe this pleasure?" Her hair was in any number of peaks and her fingers were of a reddish-brown color.

The uninvited occupants all spoke at once. "I shall have to challenge him," said the Duke. "It's my part to fight him," said Norval. "Look here, this is all of no consequence," insisted Whip. "I cannot bear it, Grandmother." Catherine fanned herself. "It was just a harmless race, Marchioness," Harriette almost whispered. But none were heard because each spoke at once.

"I collect," said the Marchioness, taking a seat by the fire, "that this is some farradiddle about the afternoon's outing. Well," she allowed none to break into her monologue, "I notice two people are missing. Don't tell me who they are," she snapped at Norval. "Do you think I don't know when my own grand-daughter is not here? Catherine, if you have a fit of the vapors, I'll disown you."

"Yes, Grandmother."

"Don't interrupt me. I'll not be interrupted. The rudeness of young people astounds me. One no sooner gets a sentence out than one is interrupted." Stern as she sounded, the Marchioness' eyes twinkled. "So, we have two young people missing in the middle of the afternoon. I cannot think that is a calamity, nor do I see it as a reason to bother me at my busiest time of day." She looked at Harriette, who could guess by the laughter in her eyes that the Marchioness had been reading a novel. "Busiest time," the Marchioness repeated. "It amazes me that five young people cannot amuse themselves without complaining that two more are not of the party. In my day, five was considered a goodly number." The Marchioness paused for breath, no one daring to break in. She savored the moment, looking from one to another as if to challenge anyone to do so. Norval opened his mouth, but before he could emit a sound, she went on. "It would seem you have not enjoyed your outing, so you had better remain here and play at cards. I should not mind joining you. Benton," she summoned the ever-faithful butler, who had been standing by at a discreet distance, "have the card tables readied."

"With all due respect, Marchioness." That lady looked at the Duke in complete surprise at his effrontery in addressing her. "We cannot concentrate at cards when your granddaughter is missing."

"So she's mine is she. Must be in trouble. She's mine every time she's in trouble."

"You do encourage her, Grandmother."

"So I do. It would seem you're all at mighty loose ends without her."

"She's disgraced," announced Norval. "I'll call the fellow out."

"She could be in danger," said the Duke gravely.

"It is Lord Effly who is apt to be in danger," Catherine snapped.

The Duke raised his quizzing glass and looked at her sharply. "You are not, then, worried about your sister's honor?"

"But she can be in no danger with Lord Effly. You expect your own sister to be safe enough with him."

The Duke did not answer this but began pacing again, his hands behind his back. Whip and Harriette drew a little apart and had trouble keeping straight faces while watching the others. Norval commenced pacing behind the Duke, and Beau, thinking this great fun, joined in behind Norval. The Duke stopped. Norval stopped. Beau sat down, scratched, and yawned. "There is no help for it," the Duke announced. "I shall fight Effly."

"That is my privilege," insisted Norval as Catherine sank onto a sofa, and Harriette went to fan her. "I am the better shot."

"I do not think that has been established." The Duke bridled.

"No offense, old fellow. Just that everyone knows it, don't you know. Effly is better than you, so you had better let me do it."

"Are you questioning my courage?"

"No, I just told you. You ain't so good as me. I thought I made that clear."

"I resent your implication."

"No implication. Damned obvious fact. Excuse me, ladies."

"There will be no duel," said the Marchioness with authority.

"I beg your pardon, Marchioness, but I am determined. Your granddaughter's honor has been be-smirched, and if no one else is concerned, *I* am. I shall call out Effly, my oldest and dearest friend."

"I'm concerned. I said I was concerned. Didn't I say, Marchioness, that I'm concerned? I'm going to call him out."

"If you will be so good as to notice, Norval, I'm dealing the cards. Whip," the Marchioness chuckled, "I like that name. Wouldn't have minded it myself once. Whip, you, Norval, and Stanfield join me. Young ladies, you can look on. There is nothing like whist to change one's mood."

There was nothing for it but to agree. Catherine remained where she was as the gentlemen seated themselves and Harriette took a place beside Whip. The Marchioness had already dealt the cards and was studying her hand. The playing commenced and went on at a dull rate, as certain players found it difficult to concentrate, for whatever reason. Whip was more than common concerned with Harriette's advice, and they had any number of conferences behind the fan of cards, while Norval muttered to himself and the Duke played silently, his visage a mask to his feelings. After an unconscionable time, during which the curtains had been drawn and the candles lit, the doors opened and in walked Julia and Lord Effly. The two truants appeared disheveled but not remorseful.

"Aha." Stanfield rose, knocking over his chair which fell on Beau, causing the poor dog to awaken in alarm. That animal, never violent, sprang up and grabbed the leg of the Duke's trousers. "Here, let me alone!"

exclaimed the Duke, attempting to free himself by stepping back. He did not remember the fallen chair, and ended on the floor, Beau on top of him, licking his face.

Whip and Harriette could not contain themselves and doubled up in laughter. Julia, attempting not to laugh, rushed to him. The wound to vanity was obviously deep and would require the most attentive ministrations. Catherine, on the other hand, hurried to Lord Effly, offering him her sympathy.

Julia's concern only added to the fire of humiliation, so that by the time the Duke had risen, he was in a worse humor than before. He walked to Effly and gave a stiff bow. "I offer you my glove, sir."

"I say, I object," put in Norval, rising from the card table.

Lord Effly looked dumbfounded. "See here, Thomas."

"No, you see here. You take a young lady to Bloomsbury. You, you compromise her, then expect that I shall not hold you to account? You must and will restore her honor, sir."

"But if we hadn't had trouble with the carriage wheel, we should have been back long ago."

"You might as well have taken her to the South Pole."

"But it is only the other side of town."

"The wrong side, Effly. The wrong side. None of the *haut ton* ever ventures there. It might as well be the South Pole."

"Look here." Lord Effly looked pale. "You surely do not mean I'm to marry her?"

"That is precisely what is expected," sputtered the Duke, only to catch himself up. "I mean . . . well, that is . . ." He sank upon a settee, looking very pale himself.

"Damnation. You cannot be serious."

"I suppose there is no help for it." The Duke held his head in his hands.

"See here," Norval intervened, "you're forgetting me. She's supposed to marry me."

"Lord Effly, I shall certainly not marry you," announced the young lady in question, ignoring Norval.

Catherine was in tears. "I, I fear you must," she sobbed. "You have ruined us all."

The Duke raised his head and looked sharply at Catherine but said nothing. The Marchioness sat with Beau on her lap and surveyed the scene. "Grandmother, do something," wailed Catherine. The Marchioness scratched Beau behind the ears. "I shall let you young people sort out your own affairs."

"But do you not see how dreadful this is?" Catherine protested.

"I see a great deal that confirms earlier suspicions," her grandmother answered. "But as everyone knows, I ain't one to meddle."

Whip and Harriette had stopped laughing and looked on wide-eyed. Julia tossed her head imperiously. "I shall certainly not marry Lord Effly. Thomas, do you hear me? I am certainly flattered to think you must force someone to marry me."

"Don't need to force *me*," said Norval.

"Who was it drove to Bloomsbury?" demanded the

Duke. "Do you never think of the consequences of your actions?"

"I shall marry no one, Thomas. No one. I am determined to be a spinster, am I not, Harriette?" Her friend merely nodded her assent. "You see, the die is cast."

"Spinster, is it? Never was told that before." Norval in his agitation pulled at the strap to his eye patch. "I should have been informed. Mother knows nothing of it, I'll be bound."

"No, Norval, I did not take your mother into my confidence."

"Should have, don't you know. This will upset her."

The Duke arose. "My second will call upon you," he said to Lord Effly.

"Under other circumstances that would have been I," said Lord Effly. "This is all ridiculous, Thomas. Whom will you ask?"

"Do you think I have no other friends?"

"Certainly not, only . . ."

"I still say it's my place to duel," Norval groused. No one answered him. "I suppose I must be your second, if you are determined to carry this through."

Catherine was furious. "Do not be so obliging, Norval."

"Oh, always like to be obliging. Think nothing of it."

"Come along then, Norval. Effly, you will hear from us." The Duke stalked from the room, and Norval obediently followed.

Lord Effly walked to the other end of the long

drawing room and dejectedly peered from the window. Catherine joined him there while Julia joined the other three. "Just think! There's to be a duel over me!"

"Isn't it romantic!" Harriette's eyes danced.

"Damned dangerous, though," said Whip.

"Yes, I suppose so. What ought we to do, Grandmama?"

The Marchioness chuckled. "I doubt that two best friends will actually shoot each other. They are good enough sportsmen to hit or miss a target at will. I think it will take a duel to wake up a certain party."

"But, Grandmama, he insists I marry Lord Effly. Did you not hear him?"

"Hear him? He startled himself with that. He is in a fine state now. Can't think but what it will do him good."

"Marchioness," Whip said, his eyes alight, "I do perceive that you never meddle."

"Quite so, young man. Now you and Harriette have a walk in the garden. I collect there are things you two might care to say to each other. I do believe Lord Effly is occupied."

The two young people needed no second invitation to depart. "Come, child," said the Marchioness when they had gone. "Let's leave these two together." She motioned toward Catherine and Lord Effly at the other end of the room.

"Grandmama, you do not suppose Thomas wants me to marry another?"

"No, child." She laughed. "I am rather certain this is the first time a man planned to fight a duel so that his

201

love must marry someone else. Don't think Stanfield ain't mighty upset. He's got himself in a pretty pickle."

"I wonder how he will work it out."

"If he's half the man I think he is, he'll find a solution. Don't look so dismayed, puss. If he don't, I will."

Julia had to laugh. "Just think, Grandmama, a duel will be fought over me. I never expected that. It is grander than my wildest dreams."

"So as to take you down to earth, puss, let me remind you that one of the gentlemen ain't so keen on marrying you."

Julia giggled. "I had forgot that. You have put me in my place. Let us pray, though, that one of the gentlemen will discover he is keen on it."

CHAPTER
FIFTEEN

Harriette knocked lightly, entered, and joined Julia, who was curled up on her huge bed. "Isn't it exciting," Harriette ventured. "The duel, I mean. Imagine, two men fighting over you."

"As Grandmama pointed out, one is not doing so willingly. It would seem neither man fighting for me wants to marry me. This must be the strangest encounter in history."

"Nevertheless, it is so romantic!" Harriette sighed.

"Yes, it is romantic. I must confess, Harriette, that I like the idea immensely. Of course, I shouldn't like it if either were hurt, but I am certain they will be careful." She laughed. "Imagine a duel in which neither party wants to hurt the other, nor does he want the girl he is dueling over."

"I am convinced you are quite wrong there, Julia. I think the plan is going splendidly. My brother is so very moody and so cross with you that it must be love."

"Yes, I am sure it must be. How can I wait until the duel? We must contrive to learn the hour and be there unseen."

"That is what I came to tell you. I spoke to Norval. They will fight tomorrow at dawn."

"I do wish duels could be fought later in the day. Dawn is so very early."

"They must escape detection. Only think, what they are doing is illegal."

"Yes, isn't it wonderful."

"And a doctor will be on hand, just in case."

Julia paled. "Oh, do not say so. Do you think one of them might get hurt?"

"It is unlikely. Though, I must say, Catherine fears the worst and is in tears."

"Yet she would never admit to us that the worst to her would be if Lord Effly were slain. Poor Catherine."

"I almost forgot. Witherspoon is downstairs waiting to see you."

"Witherspoon! Let us see what he has to say." The two girls quickly slid from the bed and hurried to the saloon below.

"Miss Julia," said Witherspoon as she entered with Harriette, "you are aware that my master is to fight Lord Effly?"

"Oh, quite. And all because of me!"

Witherspoon's features did not change, though his eyes looked a bit brighter. "A worthy cause," said that gentleman's gentleman. "However, miss, I do feel it is my duty to warn you that according to his man, Lord Effly is not feeling his best about this."

"You mean he is furious?" asked Harriette.

"Exactly so, miss. With intentions, I fear, of doing mischief to my master."

"You do not mean he intends to slay him?" asked Julia in surprise.

"*Slay* is such a definite word, Miss Julia. I prefer a less harsh term."

"For the same thing?"

"Precisely."

"But he is my brother's best friend."

"That is why he is so very angry now, Miss Harriette. Hate is only the other side of the coin of love."

"That is most profound, Witherspoon."

"I do believe, Miss Harriette, that others have made the same observation before now. It is a truth of life."

"Surely," said Harriette, "Lord Effly will relent. If he is supposed to marry me, he can hardly harm my brother."

"That we cannot know, miss."

"Oh, my," said Julia, sinking onto a settee. "I do believe I feel a trifle faint."

"Julia, you cannot faint. We depend upon you."

"Then I shall not. But I am sorely tried, Harriette. Catherine is upstairs fearing for Lord Effly, and I am here fearing for Thomas. What a dreadful situation. We must stop them."

"Stop them?" The Marchioness entered the room. "And what, child, are we to stop?"

"Why, the duel, of course."

The Marchioness nodded to Witherspoon, who gave

a crisp bow. "We shan't. Difficult enough to arrange. Can't cancel it now."

"Grandmama, Lord Effly is meaning to hurt Thomas."

"Do him good, I'd say. Wake him up a little."

"You cannot mean that."

"Not really, puss, but if I'm any judge of character, which you will all agree I am, Effly will do nothing to hurt his friend. Why, ain't you seen how the man admires Stanfield? What do you say, Witherspoon? You have a head on your shoulders."

"Now that I hear your comments, My Lady, I am inclined to agree with you."

"There you are, girls. What do you say now?"

"It would be lovely to watch them duel, and for me." Julia's smile returned.

"I should enjoy it ever so much," put in Harriette.

"But if he should be hurt . . ."

"He'll never admit how he feels about you unless pushed. You'll notice he still hasn't declared himself but insists he is engaged to Catherine. I only hope a duel is powerful enough to wake him up."

The morning of the dread affair arrived.

"Hoadly, have you ever witnessed a duel?" The Duke entered his coach that the tiger had brought round.

"No, Your Grace, and don't want to now. It don't seem the thing for you and Lord Effy to be fightin'."

"We have found a viper in our midst, Hoadly. And do stop frowning. I cannot fight with poor spirits.

Where on earth is Lord Devon? He is supposed to be handling things, and instead we must sit and wait for him."

"I hear he's a late 'un, Your Grace. Word is he ain't never been on time for a duel, but then he don't never miss a shot."

"Unfortunately, we cannot say the same thing for me, about never missing, that is."

"You're up to snuff, Your Grace."

"Thank you, Hoadly."

"Beggin' pardon, Your Grace, but I hates to be the one to drive you this mornin'."

"Hoadly! How can you have so little faith in my ability? Like a funeral coach is it? Driving me to my doom, are you?"

"Somethin' like that, Your Grace, though I might not have said it just so."

"Vipers. Vipers in every nest."

"I ain't heard of no vipers, especially in London, Your Grace. I don't think vipers is your problem this mornin'. You have enough to think on Lord Effly. He ain't a bad shot in my book."

"Damn your book, Hoadly. You are dampening my spirits."

"Don't mean to dampen nothin', Your Grace, but as me pa always said, 'It don't do to look for trouble.'"

"He said that, did he? A most original and worthy comment."

"Yes. Me pa knew what was what. 'Son,' he used to say to me—he always called me son."

"That's appropriate."

" 'Son,' he'd say, 'keep a good head on your shoulders, and you won't come out bad.' "

"You seem to have followed his advice admirably."

"I tries. It's advice you might think on yourself, Your Grace. Never did me no harm."

"Yes. Well, I hope you do not think I am close to losing my head, Hoadly."

"You did that when you said you'd fight a duel."

"I did, did I? Such impudence. I instigated the duel."

"More's the pity."

"See here, Hoadly . . . Oh, there you are, Norval. What has kept you? Do you want me to look the coward? Get in. Hoadly will drive us."

"I say, you don't look too good, Stanfield. Must be rising early, what? Well, let's get on with it."

"Hoadly." The Duke gave his command. The tiger flicked his whip, and the horses started toward the park.

Harriette and Julia had decided it would be better not to inform Catherine of the exact time and place of the duel. She would have a fit of the vapors and spoil everything. The two girls dressed hurriedly and slipped out unnoticed, Witherspoon awaiting them outside in one of the Duke's carriages. Julia had chosen her German mantle, trimmed with fur, and Harriette was none too warmly wrapped in a French shawl. Both wore demi-boots against the damp grass of the park. "I must appear my best," Julia had explained to Harriette, "for after the duel, I want to look nice when I comfort Thomas. I shall hold him in my arms, like this, his head resting on the fur of my Witz-choura."

"But that is only if he is wounded. Supposing he is not?"

"Indeed, I cannot think he will be wounded. Nevertheless, if he is, I am prepared."

"It does present a romantic scene," then Harriette scowled, "except that Norval will be there."

"Just so he does not fight. He forgets what he is about and actually becomes dangerous."

"Yes, and he is determined to fight because of you."

"We must keep well out of sight. If he sees me, he is more apt to show bravado.

"Norval is certainly not an easy one to avoid."

"How true, Harriette, even for so practiced a person as I. Witherspoon," she called to him where he sat next to the coachman, "do tell the driver to hurry."

"We are making all possible haste, miss."

"Oh, Harriette, I could not wait for today, and now I am terrified that something will go wrong."

"I, too, for my brother's sake. I cannot say I should mind too much if Lord Effly were wounded."

"For shame. I think if he had not been forced upon you, you would like him well enough. He is pleasant and except for being stuffy, he cuts quite a good figure."

"I suppose you are right, but I am reluctant to agree."

"Well, we must not wish him harm. That would be quite wicked. And only think what that would do to poor Catherine."

"Do you think my brother notices her attentions to Lord Effly?"

"I have seen him raise his quizzing glass more than once and stare at her. I cannot think that he does not notice. Yet he says nothing."

"It is certainly clear to everyone else. It amazes me that he does not cry off."

"It amazes me that *she* does not cry off. They make the strangest, most determined couple imaginable."

"What a dreadful married couple they will make, neither caring for the other."

"That is precisely what we are here to prevent. In a way I suppose we can say we are saving them."

"Julia, you do have a way of putting things. I am sure Mrs. Radcliffe herself could do no better."

"Why doesn't the coachman go faster? I could have had us there by now."

"Not without adding some white hair to Witherspoon's head." Both girls laughed.

Soon the coach drew up to a covering of trees. Witherspoon helped the girls to alight and led them to a small opening in the thicket. Beyond, on a green knoll, stood the Duke and Norval, both looking the picture of gloom. Hoadly stood at a distance with the horses and carriage. Several yards away a coach had only now deposited Lord Effly and his second. It would not be long before the duel would commence.

"Only look at how handsome Thomas looks," Julia whispered to Harriette. "I am so glad he wore his maroon jacket with dove pants. It quite becomes him."

"I think it rather ominous, as if it were the color of blood."

"Do not say so." Julia said this so loudly that Witherspoon had to quiet her for fear of detection. "Only remember, miss," he remonstrated, "if you are caught spying, it is quite a different thing from my being caught and also found to be the one who has brought you. This very morning my career as gentleman's gentleman may come to an abrupt conclusion."

"Poor Witherspoon." Julia was contrite. "We shan't let you down."

"Yes, miss. That is what I said to myself. She is not giddy like other young girls."

"I can tell from the look on your face that you think I was giddy just now. I shall take your hint, Witherspoon, and be very cautious."

"Thank you, miss. That gratifies me. You, Miss Harriette, I have always depended upon."

"Yes, indeed, Witherspoon. You will find us very staunch and brave."

Witherspoon showed the rare flicker of a smile and resumed his watch. Norval and Lord Effly's second, who was unknown to the girls, met without the two principals in order to attempt to settle the thing amicably and if not that, to define terms. Apparently they could come to no agreement, for Lord Effly's second kept shaking his head and scowling. Finally, Norval turned to the Duke, shrugged his shoulders and walked back to the pistol case.

"I thought they might give the whole thing up," whispered Harriette.

"I, too. Now they will actually fight. I wonder if there is any scene so dramatic as this, even in Miss Austen's latest work."

"I think not. I am goose bumps all over."

"So am I. If this does not turn out as it should, I shall lead a single life and become an authoress."

"I think I shall join you. Once one has gone through this much, one is almost obliged to set it down."

"I agree."

"Do be still, young ladies. You will have us discovered yet."

"Sorry, Witherspoon," they both whispered. But the main actors in the drama seemed not to notice.

Each man selected a Manton pistol. Norval, who looked unhappily like an undertaker in his black jacket and eye patch, attempted to advise the Duke.

"Harriette, I do not think I can stand this. I must get them to call it off."

Harriette held her friend back. "You cannot stop them now. Were you to appear, they would be much more apt to hurt each other."

"Do calm yourself, Miss Julia. It will all be over soon."

"That is what I fear." Julia hugged her friend, then almost sneezed as the feather on Harriette's hat tickled her nose.

The two men stood back to back, pistols down. They commenced pacing. "Oh, no!" exclaimed Julia as they continued past twelve yards.

"Quiet, miss," said Witherspoon.

"But Lord Effly is the better shot and has a far better chance at twenty-five yards."

"That, miss, we have no control over."

"It is all my fault."

"Do not despair, Julia. Surely, they will not hurt one another."

"Now I am not so sure."

"Oh, do not say so."

The duelers now stood twenty-five yards apart. The green of the park and the soft early morning light seemed in direct contrast to the thought of dueling or death. A bird warbled. Its mate answered. Both men checked to see that their pistols were cocked. At Norval's command they turned, showing only their side view so as to be poorer targets. "I shall raise my handkerchief," Norval was saying. "When I drop it, shoot."

It seemed to take Norval forever to remove a white handkerchief from his jacket pocket and raise it into the air. Both duelers stood poised, not moving a muscle. The onlookers, as well, scarcely breathed. Then all too soon, the handkerchief left Norval's fingers and fell lightly, blown by a soft breeze. There was the crash of a pistol and another, almost simultaneously, as Julia and Harriette screamed. Then all was silent.

Suddenly the others were making their way to the Duke, who lay on the ground. The doctor was beside him, shooing everyone away.

"You have killed him," Julia cried, beating upon Lord Effly with her fists as he attempted to keep her from the Duke.

"I should never have hit him if I had not been startled by screams. What are you two doing here?"

"You are too good a shot for that. I don't believe you."

"It's true, right enough." Norval came up to them.

"I'll wager you was hiding your eyes like a moonling, or you'd have known. You were hiding them, weren't you?"

Julia nodded.

"Damned fool thing to do. Lord Effly was far of the mark until your screaming jolted him. Just like you, Julia, to mix things up."

"And did my brother try to hit you?"

"He fired into the air, Harriette."

"*I* should have been fighting you," Norval went on. "You'd be a dead man now, Effly."

"I do not doubt that, Norval. I am much obliged to Stanfield for insisting on the fight."

"He is dying, and you stand here making foolish comments."

"He ain't dying, Julia," said Norval. "Shot just grazed his arm."

"He is lying on the ground while the doctor checks his arm," said Lord Effly, scornfully. "If you'd been watching, which is what I presume you came to do, you'd know that he stumbled and fell."

"That is so unromantic," said Harriette.

"Ain't nothing romantic about a cold morning and two people firing at each other," complained Norval.

"But it is supposed to be," put in Julia. "Life is never the way it is supposed to be." She sighed.

"What are you girls doing here?" bawled the Duke from where he sat as the doctor now rigged a sling for his arm to relieve the pressure. "Have you two goose-caps been here all along?"

"He certainly sounds all right." Julia had to smile. "I

fear, Harriette, we are in trouble again." She went over to Thomas. "Poor Thomas, does your arm hurt very much?"

"Do not 'poor Thomas' me. What are you two doing here?"

"If two people are going to fight over me, I certainly have the right to be on hand."

"Over you? You wicked little beast. You rogue. Fight over you? I was upholding your family honor, a thing you take too lightly. Fight over you, indeed." The Duke struggled to his feet, the doctor fussing over him. "Can you imagine that, Effly. She thinks we were fighting over her."

"Over a mere girl? Two friends falling out over a mere girl? Ridiculous."

"Julia," announced Harriette, "I think we should leave immediately. There is a certain person here whom I do not care to talk to."

"Damme," said Norval, "you *was* fighting over Julia. I wanted to duel, and you wouldn't have it. Now you change your story. It won't fadge, Stanfield. I'll call you both out. You'll be fought over if you like, Julia."

"Thank you, Norval. At least *you* are a gentleman."

"Mother will be glad to know you've said that."

"There will be no more dueling," said the Duke gruffly. "You young ladies have had quite enough romance in your lives for one day. And my arm feels as though it is on fire."

"Sorry about that, old friend." Lord Effly put his arm around the Duke's shoulder.

215

"Couldn't be helped with those two on the scene."

"Come, Harriette, we must be going," Julia said icily. "Witherspoon, will you see us safely home?"

"Certainly, miss."

"See here," insisted Norval, "I'll see them home. Stanfield, if you wasn't wounded, I'd plant you a facer. You can't fight for a lady, then say you haven't done it. And you two shouldn't be friends any more. This should have been a permanent falling out."

"I quite agree, Norval," said Harriette. "Let us go now."

The two ladies, accompanied by Norval, took the Duke's carriage home, much to Hoadly's disgust; and Witherspoon was left to return with his master. The girls left the group so abruptly that they did not see the laughter in both Effly's and Stanfield's eyes.

"Do you think they were satisfied, Witherspoon?"

"Yes, indeed, Your Grace." Even the staunch Witherspoon had to smile.

"If those two hadn't done that damnable screaming, I should have been saved this sore arm."

"Sorry about that, Stanfield. Nerves, don't you know."

"Quite. I am certainly glad you talked some sense into me, Effly. I can see that you and Catherine are in love."

"And I finally made you admit to loving Julia."

"But do you think she loves me in return, or is she just infatuated with romance?"

"Have no fear, Your Grace," said Witherspoon. "If I may venture to say so, she puts you before even romance."

"Well, the little vixen must learn not to manage people's affairs."

"I fear, Your Grace, that is a lesson she may never learn."

"Not even after this duel?"

"Stanfield, you must take her as you find her."

The Duke had to laugh. "I find her rather remarkable. I tell you, Effly, my life will not be a boring one."

"But what of the Whip fellow, Your Grace?"

"You saw Harriette with him. I suppose he will do. Now let us get back to breakfast and some dry clothes. What one will not do for love."

CHAPTER
SIXTEEN

"The Duke of Stanfield, Miss Julia." Benton entered the long drawing room and announced the guest.

"I shall not see him, Benton. Tell the Duke that I am not at home."

"But you are at home, and I am already in."

Benton bowed and closed the doors on the pair.

"I cannot think that you wish to see me. Catherine is upstairs. I shall have her called."

"I do wish to see you. Look at my arm in a sling. Are you not responsible?"

"Not according to you and Lord Effly."

"I must say, had you not gone to Bloomsbury . . ."

"Had *you* not called attention to our delay, no one would have noticed. Now you have hurt my good name and humiliated me. I think you had better go up to Catherine. That is, if she cares to see you."

"Am I in disgrace in that quarter as well?"

"I believe so. As a matter of fact, Lord Effly is with her now, comforting her."

"I have no doubt of that. And may I not comfort you?"

"Great comfort, to blame me for your wound. I am sorry for it, but it is your own fault. At any rate, I must supervise the packing."

"Packing!"

"Yes, I am returning to the country, where I shall study the philosophers with Papa and write my memoirs."

"So young to be writing memoirs." The Duke's lips quivered.

"I have been busy living life and know much."

"I do not like to bring this up, but from what I have seen in the samples you have given me to read, you do not write very well."

"That is of no consequence. The tragic content will take precedence over a faulty style."

"I suppose I shall be in your book?"

"I suppose so."

"You are sure to house us all in Gothic ruins."

"One must suit the background to the characters."

"And what of your study of mesmerism?"

"I shall doubtless continue. I have been reasonably successful. One cannot help difficult subjects."

"And have you had those?"

"One, sir. Only one."

"Would you not like to practice on me again?"

Julia sighed and went to the window. "I think not."

"But why?"

"I am not in the mood. Nor do I have as much faith in it as I once did."

"You, Julia, the Marchioness' granddaughter, admitting defeat?"

She got out a very soft and quavering, "Yes."

"I am sorry to hear that. I should very much like the pain in my arm to lessen, and I was hoping you could help."

"Are you in pain? I am sorry for it. I do not think, though, that I can help."

"You can but try."

"Very well. Be seated."

The Duke did as he was bade, and soon Julia was intoning her commands, though she forgot to use her special voice and sounded truly dejected. "Now you are in a deep sleep. Your arm no longer pains you. The wound is healing fast and you feel no pain." She paused. "Oh, what is the use," she said to herself. "I shall count from five to one. When I reach one, you will open your eyes and you will feel no pain."

"But my eyes are open."

She turned, startled.

"Why did you not give me any more suggestions?"

"Clearly it would have been useless. You did not go into a trance. I wonder why."

The Duke merely smiled his broad, mischievous smile.

"You were in a trance before. I mean . . ."

He laughed. "No, dear Julia, I must confess I have never been in a trance."

"You have tricked me."

"And *you* have tricked *me*."

"I think you are despicable."

"I think we deserve each other."

"And what of Catherine? You have ignored her these many weeks and have not even noticed that she and Lord Effly make a devoted pair."

"On the contrary," his eyes twinkled, "I have been all too aware. Your mesmerism has done wonders for me. And if it did not put me in a trance, it opened my eyes to my surroundings. You are a very accomplished practitioner."

Julia blushed. "You jest, surely. I have made an utter fool of myself."

"No, indeed. You have taught me much, not the least of which is to laugh at life a little more often." He drew her gently to him and kissed her.

"Oh Thomas, Thomas. After the duel I had given you up for good."

He laughed. "My dear, do you not think you deserved our little charade after all your romanticizing and manipulating?"

"It was only because I love you."

"I know that. And it did convince Catherine that she must cry off and marry Effly."

"I am so glad. And you approve of Whip for Harriette?"

"I surrender completely to you. I shall never cross you again. It is far too much trouble and can be rather painful." He glanced at his arm. She laughed.

"I am so happy you understand that it is useless to defy me." But she could barely speak, for without a command, he was crushing her to him, the power of

221

him making her tremble. She felt his breath on her face as he gently kissed her forehead, her eyes, her nose, her cheeks. His kisses were warm and possessive. Finally, he took her mouth, his tongue parting her lips, exploring and hinting at greater pleasures to follow. His hand, buried in her golden curls, now traced the nape of her neck, then sought out the contours of her ripe figure, easily accessible through the thin muslin dress she wore, as she gave herself up to the waves of desire that surged through her.

At first they did not hear the cough. When it sounded again, and rather loudly, they parted in some confusion.

"It is only I," said the Marchioness. "Glad to find you here, Stanfield. I see you two are friends again."

The both looked disconcerted. "I assure you," said the Duke.

"And I assure you, Stanfield, that it's about time you knew what you were about. I had begun to think the accident had addled your brain. Well, I shall leave you. Come along, Beau." She withdrew with the dog, shutting the doors behind her with a snap.

She looked down at Beau, a smile on her face. "I think we have trapped a fine thoroughbred for my puss, Beau. If she will be clever, as I think she will, hold the ribbons skillfully and not keep him in check, he'll handle quite well."

She walked up the stairs, her smile lingering. "Beau, we are, like it or not, members of society. When one lives in the world, one must use the tools of the world. I want her to stay happy and independent. As a Duchess, she may do pretty much as she likes and be thought witty and original. If she were the wife of a mere knight or baronet, she would be thought daring and at worst eccentric. However, if she were the wife of an untitled gentleman, her behavior would be considered unacceptable. Of course, her money would always keep her in a position to be thought merely silly, whatever her activities. But having the power of a title as well as her fortune, she will hold society's two gods in her hands and will always receive acceptance and even praise."

They reached her bedchamber. The Marchioness picked up the latest Maria Edgeworth novel while Beau yawned and fell asleep.

Love—the way you want it!

Candlelight Romances